Riding the Waves

Riding the Waves

Theresa Tomlinson

Macmillan Publishing Company   New York

Maxwell Macmillan International
New York   Oxford   Singapore   Sydney

For Tom, Rosie, Joe, and Sam,
with love

First American edition 1993
Copyright © 1990 by Theresa Tomlinson

Macmillan Publishing Company is part of the
Maxwell Communication Group of Companies.

Macmillan Publishing Company
866 Third Avenue, New York, NY 10022

Originally published by Julia MacRae Books, London, England
Printed in the United States of America

10 9 8 7 6 5 4 3 2 1

The text of this book is set in 11 point Sabon.
Book design by Constance Ftera

Library of Congress Cataloging-in-Publication Data
Tomlinson, Theresa.
    Riding the waves / Theresa Tomlinson. — 1st American ed.
        p.   cm.
    Summary: In an English seaside town, Matt befriends an elderly
woman who helps him fulfill his dream of surfing and learn
to accept his having been adopted.
    ISBN 0-02-789207-7
    [1. Old age—Fiction. 2. Surfing—Fiction. 3. Adoption—Fiction.
4. England—Fiction.] I. Title.
    PZ7.T5977Ri 1993   [Fic]—dc20   92-3942

NOTE TO THE READER

This book is set in northern England, in the seaside county of Cleveland. The way people live there is changing, as it is in parts of the United States. Industries like steel and coal mining that used to employ many people have shut down, and some people, like the main character's father in this story, have to go south to London to find work.

Although the U.S. and England share some problems, life in England can be different; people don't always use the same words. In England, people go to the "chemist's shop" instead of the drugstore, eat "chips" rather than French fries, and stand in a "queue," not a line. One can figure out other different words—and customs—as they come up in the story.

Students in England go to what is called a "comprehensive school," which is like a combined junior high and high school, beginning at age eleven or twelve. There they study for the GSCE (General Certificate in Secondary Education), which they earn after taking a series of exams at age sixteen. In PE (gym, or physical education), football—which Americans call soccer—is a favorite sport, rather than baseball, "American football," or basketball.

Surfing, which is common on America's coasts, is not very common in England. The North Sea is so cold that surfers must wear wet suits all year round when they are riding the waves.

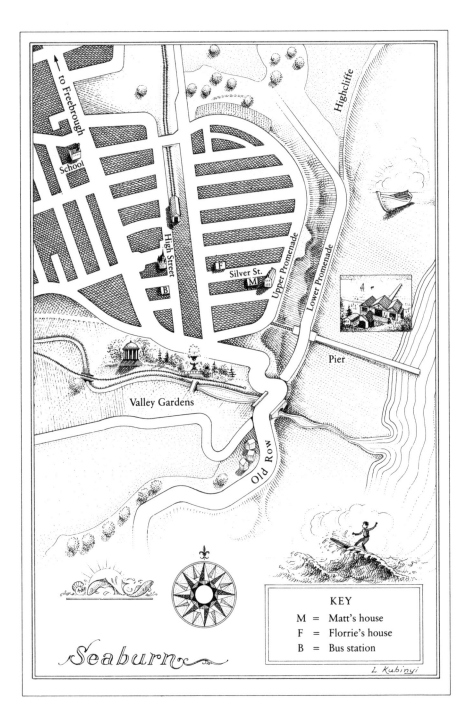

CHAPTER 1

Matt crouched in the muddy hollow, halfway down the grassy bank. From there he could see the bottom promenade, the pier, and the sea. The lower half of his body was hidden by the dip. He leaned out over the edge, the wind whipping his hair back from his face so that the tip of his nose turned pink. He stretched his neck to get the best view possible, without them seeing him.

He needn't have worried; they had no interest in him. All they lived for was the white, pumping surf. They came here every afternoon through spring and autumn, when the waves were at their strongest. Young men dressed in crazy-colored wet suits, cutting through the breakers on their surfboards, shooting plumes of white spray high into the sky. Despite the steelworks belching gray smoke in the distance, they turned the freezing stretch of northern sea into a fabulous place of adventure.

Matt adored them. To him they were film-star heroes, even though the sands were littered with papers and the sea was floating with stuff from the sewage pipe.

*   *   *

He looked at his watch and sighed. He could have stayed there forever watching them. Closing his eyes for a moment, he saw himself riding the waves. It didn't matter that it was cold and dirty hiding in the hollow, when he could see things like that.

He looked down at the cardboard box full of fruit that he'd dumped down in the mud. It looked funny there, all out of place. It was carefully arranged. Three delicious-looking plums on top and a nice bunch of grapes, with cellophane wrapping to keep it all neat. You could see that it was a present. Matt laughed. He wanted to leave it there. A present for the wild men on their surfboards. An offering for the hungry waves.

He picked it up, rubbing a smudge of mud off the side. It was no good, he'd have to go and do it. It wasn't for the sea or the surfing men, it was a gift from the First Year at Seaburn Bay Comprehensive School, and he was supposed to deliver it to some old biddy who used to know his grandmother. He climbed carefully out of the dip and picked at the specks of dirt on his trousers. He'd better get it done. Someone just might check up on him, and then he'd be in for it.

Matt pressed the doorbell of number twenty-four, balancing the basket on his knee. He stood back from the door and glanced over his shoulder. She might not be in. He looked around once more to see if any of his mates were in the street. He'd die if they saw him doing this, even though they all had to do it, too.

It was all right for them; most of them had grannies. That sorted it all out. They just handed the basket over when they next went to visit. They'd probably get their mothers to do it for them.

Matt shifted his weight from one foot to the other, as if doing that would make him more comfortable. He was supposed to call this old woman Auntie Florrie. But she wasn't his auntie, and he felt like a stupid Red Riding Hood standing there on the doorstep.

They hadn't seen much of Florrie since his gran had died. It had been his mother's idea that Florrie should be presented with a basket of fruit.

"Can't you do it?" Matt had pleaded. He could usually get around his mother, but for once she'd been firm.

He kicked the toe of his shoe into the messy, rutted tarmac in front of the doorstep, then backed away toward the gate. He wasn't going to hang around all day; but as he turned to go, a light clicked on in the hall. There was a shuffling sound, then the scraping of locks and bolts.

He sighed and went back to the steps. At least he would get it over with. He'd only have had to come back again if he didn't do it now.

The door opened just wide enough for Florrie's face to appear in the space. She was plump and pink-cheeked, but she had a suspicious, rather worried look about her.

"Yes?"

He held out the basket.

"From Seaburn Comprehensive. The harvest festival."

Florrie stared at the basket, frowning. "Don't eat fruit."

Matt sighed. What was he supposed to do now?

Florrie sniffed. "Don't need charity, either."

She looked as though she was going to shut the door. Matt had a sudden urge to sling the rotten basket into her hedge.

But then the door stopped, opened up again. Florrie screwed up her eyes. "I know you."

"Yes. You knew my gran, I think."

"Joyce. Joyce Western. Aye, a good friend she was, and I do know you, 'course I do. Seen you whizzing down the street on that big roller-skate thing."

"Oh, skateboard, you mean."

"Hmm. Dangerous little devil you are."

Matt hunched his shoulders and put his hand out for the gate.

"Wait a bit. Got to give that away to some old so-and-so, haven't you?"

Matt jumped. She'd spoken his very thoughts.

"Do you like fruit?"

He nodded.

"Better come in then. Save you trailing around."

She moved back from the door with an awkward grunt, holding it open just a fraction wider, so there was hardly room for Matt to squeeze through. He hesitated.

"Come on, don't mind me. Get yourself in." Matt stepped into the hall, and she gave the front door a shove. She was a small woman in a clean, flowery dress. Her hair was white and brushed smooth. She looked smart and tidy, but as she turned, she gave another painful grunt. That bothered Matt.

Florrie saw the embarrassment in his face.

"Nowt wrong," she said. "Not really. Had a fall, about two weeks since."

"Oh. . . ." Matt wondered what he was supposed to say. "Looks bad."

"What?" She shouted it rather suddenly and made him jump.

"It looks bad, I said," Matt repeated, wishing he hadn't said anything.

"Oh, well. I'm fine. Nearly better anyway. Bruised all down my back, that's all."

"Shouldn't you get the doctor?"

"Certainly not. He's no good, isn't Dr. Sutherland. Used to come in my chip shop when he was just a lad. I'm getting myself better, I am. You go into the kitchen. Straight ahead."

Matt walked down the passage, feeling like a trapped animal. Florrie followed him slowly, grasping at the walls and doorway.

"Put it down there. Yes . . . on the table."

"Um. You said you didn't like fruit, though."

"Me? No. Nasty, messy stuff. Full of sticky juice that dribbles down your arms. You like it, though, so sit yourself down on that chair and you can eat it. Don't want it wasted."

"Oh."

He pulled the chair out and sat down, but he knew that this wasn't the way it was supposed to be. The vicar hadn't meant this when he said that "charity begins at home." Still, Matt couldn't think what to say and he felt as though it would be bad manners to point out that she'd got it all wrong.

Florrie passed him down a china plate from the sideboard. "You get a knife from the table drawer. Now fetch that clean tea towel. Get going, then. Start with the grapes."

Grapes were a rare enough treat, and there didn't seem to be any point in hanging around. He quickly polished off the grapes and moved onto the plums and oranges.

Florrie pressed her knuckles on the table and groaned as she lowered herself into a chair. She recovered as soon as she'd sat down.

Matt worried about spitting the pips out and tried to do it with as little fuss as possible, lining them up neatly on the side of the plate.

"Now," said Florrie. "Tell me what's been going on in Seaburn."

Matt's mind went blank. He didn't know what was the right sort of thing to say. Dribbly pear juice ran down his chin as he tried to tell her about the harvest festival at school, and how the vicar had preached about charity. Charity was to be their motto.

"Charity?" Florrie snapped.

Matt remembered miserably that she didn't approve of charity.

"Don't tell me all that," she said. "I get all that from Miss Mawson. I couldn't care less what the vicar said. Give me the gossip. I've picked up nothing for the last two weeks. Is that new PE teacher at your school still meeting the curate at lunchtimes? Is Mrs. Simpson really having her sixth? What happened about that husband of hers, drunk and disorderly down on the pier?"

Matt was appalled. Nice old ladies weren't supposed to enjoy all the latest scandal like that. He couldn't even guess how she knew about the PE teacher; they'd only just noticed themselves that something was going on there. Still . . . everyone knew about the goings-on of the Simpson family, and how Alf Simpson had punched the young bobby who'd tried to arrest him so that they'd both ended up in the sea.

Florrie's cheeks were flushed and her eyes snapped with interest.

"Go on," she said. "Give us the gossip. I'd rather have that than a basket of fruit."

Matt shrugged his shoulders. It felt all wrong, but again it didn't seem polite not to do what she told him. He launched into all the latest on the Simpson family, and as she encouraged him with nods and wicked grins, he found himself warming to his story and forgetting that she was not one of his school-yard friends.

"Well, fancy that," said Florrie when he paused for breath. "I do feel better for hearing all that."

"I don't think I can manage all the apples." His stomach had become decidedly tight.

"Stuff 'em in your pocket then. No one will know. Now get that dishcloth. No, no, squeeze it out first. Has Linda taught you nowt? There . . . that's it. Wipe the table. There. There's a patch of sticky stuff."

Fussy old bat, Matt thought.

He did as he was told, but moved over to the door as soon as he could, saying that he must go.

"Don't you go telling your mother that I'm badly." Florrie wagged a finger at his nose. "I don't want her coming fussing around here. Treating me like a baby. I've enough of that."

"Okay." Matt had had enough of her, too, and he wanted to get out.

"On your way, lad. You've done your duty."

She touched his shoulder as he passed her.

"I'd be glad for you to pop in again, you know."

He made an unrecognizable sound in the back of his throat, and went.

No chance of that, he thought. He'd better things to do than think up nasty stories for bossy old women.

He slammed her gate, then stood for a moment on the pavement, listening to the sounds of her locking up. He set off down the street, grinning to himself now. Grinning because it was over, and it hadn't been so terrible. He wondered how the vicar's face would look if he'd seen him there, stuffing his face with the fruit.

He stopped. Had she said that she'd not been out for two weeks? How was she getting shopping and things like that? Oh well, that was nothing to do with him. He poked a can out of the gutter with his toe and kicked it down the street. He certainly wasn't going back there again.

CHAPTER 2

Matt kicked the can all the way down Silver Street. His shoulders drooped at the thought of the evening ahead. He'd got rotten science homework that he couldn't understand. His mother would be busy and anxious, working hard to please the last trickle of elderly paying guests who came in the autumn for the cheaper rates.

Winter used to be the best time of the year as far as Matt was concerned. He didn't mind it being wet and cold, he just enjoyed the comfortable feeling of being a family again. Having the house to themselves. The freedom to spread his gear around wherever he wanted. Coming down to breakfast in his pajamas, and his mother not bothering if he left the bathtub dirty.

This winter wasn't going to be like that, though. This winter was going to be miserable, with his dad away, working in London.

He stood on the can and crushed it. It all seemed so stupid. There was the Grand Seaburn Hotel at the bottom of their street, crumbling away on the seafront. It was a magnificent building, one of the oldest and finest in Seaburn Bay, but it

15

stood empty and derelict. It just cried out to be fixed up, but there was his dad having to go off to London to find building work there.

Matt had walked round to the Grand with his dad last time he'd been home. They'd climbed the stone steps that had dandelions growing between the cracks and they'd gone peering in through the windows, the ones that weren't boarded up. They had looked in on a strange world of vast, empty rooms with fancy tiled floors that were cracked and filthy. There were curly, wrought-iron staircases, and ceilings so high that they couldn't be seen clear. Just caverns of darkness, with flakes of plaster drifting down in the dust.

"Could it be made posh again?" Matt had asked his dad.

"Oh, aye." His father's hard fingertips had flexed on the splintering window frame. "Structure's sound enough. They built 'em to last. There's a deal of work there, but it could all be made good. The door frames are sound, and the doors, too. They just need stripping down and painting up. That plaster molding would have to come down, though, too much damage there. Shame; it's quality molding, done by hand. It could be replaced. Now look, Matt. Those hardwood floors would come up lovely if you stripped and polished them. It's the way they laid them, you see."

His dad turned away, trailing his hand along the carved stone balcony, patting it gently, as though he loved it.

"Away home, lad," he'd said. "It's no use me mooching around here all night. Not when I've got to be up early and off to London in the morning."

Matt turned in at his gateway and kicked the garden sign that said SEAVIEW GUEST HOUSE—VACANCIES. Vacancies!

That sign had said "vacancies" all through the summer. The visitors just weren't coming to Seaburn Bay, not like they used to. They went off to Spain or Italy now, and who could blame them? He pushed the fading hydrangeas aside and went around to the back.

The smell of beef casserole warmed him as he opened the door. At least the meals were good while they still had the guests. He wished that he wasn't quite so full of fruit.

"Hi, Matt. Had a good day?" His mother called her usual greeting.

"Fine." He always said that. Even if he'd been punched in the head or kicked in the ribs, or given detention or even sent to the Head. He still said "fine." For some reason, he could never tell his mother if things were bad at school.

"Late, aren't you?"

"Went to Florrie's. Gave her the fruit."

"Oh, did you, love? I'm glad about that. I bet she was pleased, wasn't she?"

He opened his mouth to explain how he'd ended up eating the fruit, then realized how complicated that was going to be, and didn't bother.

"Yes. I think she was pleased." He smiled to himself, feeling as though he had become an unwilling conspirator, sharing silly secrets with Florrie. "We've got to talk to some old person for our history homework next week."

"Oh . . . talk about what, love?"

"Got to ask them what their school was like. What kind of lessons they did, and did they get hit with a cane. That sort of thing."

"Well, Florrie would be ideal for that. She's got a sharp enough mind, and I'm sure she'd have plenty to tell you."

"I'm sure she would." Matt pulled a face. "I'm not going knocking on doors again, though. No need to. Teacher's fixed it for us to go to the old people's club after school next Wednesday. Nobody wants to do it, but I suppose we'll have to."

"Well. All I can say is that I wish we'd had that sort of homework when I was at school. All we had was pages of notes to copy up. Seemed like that, anyway." She piled up the pillowcases that she'd been folding and smoothed them flat with her hands, looking vague and thoughtful. Then she shook her head, bringing herself back to the present. "Anyway, Florrie goes to that club. I've seen her outside the church hall, chatting on to the old men."

"Ah, but—" Matt remembered that he was not supposed to let on that Florrie had fallen. "But she'll not want to talk to me, not when she's got all the old men."

"Oh, I think she likes to talk to everyone, does Florrie. She's always been one for having a bit of a gossip."

Matt nodded and grinned to himself.

Although the stew tasted as good as it smelled, Matt couldn't eat much. He helped his mother serve up the meal to the guests, but they made a fuss over him, and he went blushing back into the kitchen, saying that he'd do the washing up as long as he didn't have to go into that dining room.

"Ey, Matt. They're only trying to be friendly to you. These autumn holiday-makers, they're often the nicest. I know it's hardly worth it for the money, but they do appreciate what you do. No complaints from them."

Matt clattered the pots in the sink. "Got to get my homework done. I've got some science that I can't do. Wish Dad was here."

His mother sighed. "I wish I could help you, love, but I can't even understand the questions."

It was the silence of the late evening that really got to Matt. That was the time when his dad used to get back from work. He would land up in the kitchen, starving hungry and covered in plaster and muck. Then it would be all noise and rushing around to get him cleaned up and sorted out.

Now, Matt and his mother sat quietly watching the telly, and Matt felt a great empty space there at the end of the day.

Wayne Smithson shoved Matt with his elbow and nipped his own nose.

"It'll stink, you know. Stink of old biddies."

"Yeah," Matt agreed.

"They do stink, you know. My gran stinks, and her house stinks, too."

"Ey. What does it smell of?"

"Dunno really. Just yuck! Don't see why we have to do this anyway. Waste of time. Ey? Waste of time."

"Yeah."

"Let's have a bit of quiet and manners." It was Mrs. Teesdale, the new history teacher, who'd brought these peculiar new ideas with her. She turned around to check that everyone was there.

As they went up the steps to the church hall, they could hear the faint clatter of teacups and low buzz of conversation.

"Right. All ready? Got your notebooks? Now, just be polite and friendly, and you'll probably enjoy yourselves."

As she pulled open the door, a great noise came bursting out, surrounding them. Matt caught his breath. The room was alive with color and sound. The atmosphere was more what he'd expect of the youth club than the over-sixties. There were faces he recognized, friends of his gran. They'd often stop him in the street and make him embarrassed by fussing over the way he'd grown, but apart from that they'd seemed harmless enough.

Here they were different. They filled the hall. They took it over. They had turned into a gang—talking loudly, laughing, pointing, waving their arms about. They were a cheerful, noisy, terrifying gang.

Matt moved closer to Wayne. The other kids went suddenly quiet. Then the vicar—it was the same one who'd sent them off distributing fruit—came over to their teacher.

"Come in, come in. Nice to see you all. Here comes the contingent from the Comprehensive." He announced it to the people around him, laughing at his own little joke, but nobody took any notice.

Matt suddenly wished that he hadn't come. Tracey Maitland was sent to sit with an enormously fat woman who had a double chin. Matt's eyes flew from face to face. He was looking for someone, searching for a particular face.

Wayne was taken by the vicar to meet a bald-headed man who leaned forward on a stick, cupping his hand to his ear, shouting at Wayne to speak up.

Panic rose in Matt. He turned his head and stretched his neck, searching into the corners for one particular face. Then it dawned on him. What was he doing? The face he was looking for was Florrie's, and she wouldn't be there. She couldn't be there, he knew that.

"Miss?" He touched the teacher's arm. "My Auntie Florrie. I've remembered that she isn't coming today. I can go to her house. I'll do that, shall I, miss?"

Mrs. Teesdale frowned at him, irritated, but then she turned to smile at the vicar, who'd returned to her side.

"I thought you hadn't been able to find anyone to interview, Matthew. That's why we've come here."

"No . . . well. I thought my auntie would be here, but she isn't." He nodded his head, trying to believe his own story. "I can go to her house . . . now."

She frowned again, still puzzled, but then gave up. "All right. Give me her name and address, then you can go."

Matt walked to the top of Silver Street in a daze. He turned the corner and then stopped.

What on earth was he doing? He'd sworn that he wouldn't go round to Florrie's again. It was just that suddenly she'd seemed less scary than that gabbling gang in the church hall.

He stared out to the distant gray sea that appeared to flow past the bottom of the street. You couldn't see the steep bank that stretched from the top promenade to the bottom promenade. For a moment, he wondered whether he dare chuck the whole thing and go climbing down the bank. He'd snuggle into his special place, behind the old chalets, all secret and sheltered. He'd crouch there, watching the pier, waiting for the surfers to arrive in their vans.

It was no good. There'd only be trouble when it came to reporting back to Mrs. Teesdale. He hauled himself back to Silver Street and faced up to what he had to do. He pulled his notepad and pen from his pocket and walked down to Florrie's house. He pressed the doorbell firmly and stood back to listen for the scraping of the bolts.

CHAPTER 3

The doorbell rang, and Florrie's duster paused in its feverish journey around the porcelain shepherds and silver-framed photographs that lived on her front-room mantelpiece.

"Aha. Miss Mawson herself."

Florrie eased the crick in her neck and waggled her shoulders as the iron tension of the battle of the housework faded for a moment.

"Aye well, shouldn't complain. Gets my shopping done, doesn't she?"

She went into the kitchen and carefully put her duster away, refusing to be hurried. She untied her cotton apron and hung it on its peg by the back door.

The bell rang again, but Florrie stopped by the mirror in the hall to pat her hair into place.

"You can wait, Miss Mawson. Plenty of time for your good deeds when I've sorted myself out. Not having it all round Seaburn that Florrie's letting herself go."

Satisfied at last, she moved toward the door. She peered through the stained-glass window, her hand shaking as she stretched up to reach the bolt at the top of the door.

"Not sure it is Miss Mawson. No hat . . . can't be her."

She bent down to tug at the bolt at the bottom, then stood back, pulling the door with a grunt. It only opened a few inches, then stuck. The gap was just wide enough for her to look through into the porch.

"Oh. It's you."

Matt stood on the doorstep, holding his notepad and pen.

"I didn't think I'd be seeing you again. Couldn't wait to get out, you couldn't."

Matt nodded agreement, then panicked. "Oh no. Didn't mean that."

Florrie laughed, her mouth wide open. "I know what you meant. Well, I thought it was Miss Mawson—you know, her from the church. She fetches my shopping for me."

There was an awkward silence, and Matt tried hard to think what it was that he was supposed to do.

"Er . . . can I interview you?"

"What? Interview me?"

"Yes . . . please. It's for school. It's our history homework. Got to interview somebody who went to school before the war."

"War? Which war?"

Matt stared at his notebook, as though it might magically give him the answer. "Dunno which war."

"Well, I was a baby in the first war, so I expect it must be the second one."

Matt nodded.

"Better come in, then."

Silly old bag, thought Matt as he squeezed through the tiny space. Why doesn't she open her door properly like any sensible person would?

He followed Florrie into her front room and watched her broad back, waiting for the awkward movements. They didn't come. She moved easily.

"Your back's better."

"It is. It's fine. I told you I could get myself better. I don't need doctors. Now, don't sit on the rose brocade, that's my best. You can sit there, on the blue velvet, but don't touch anything. I've just got it all sorted and polished."

Her words filled Matt with worry. Every surface was covered with delicate ornaments. There were dancing pottery figures, cut-glass bowls, patterned china teacups. They all looked as though they'd smash as soon as you breathed on them.

Then he noticed something else about the room. He sniffed hard. A memory that had almost gone came flooding back to him.

"I can smell something."

"What? A smell? A smell in my house?"

"Oh no—I didn't mean—It's a good smell." He tried to explain fast. "It makes me think of someone. It makes me think of . . . my gran. Her house smelled like this."

Florrie's face softened. "Oh, well. Now I know what you mean. Smells like Joyce's house used to. Lavender wax, that's what it is. We used to get it from Mr. Welford's, before they opened the new supermarket."

Matt touched a white embroidered cover that hung over the back of a chair.

"She had these, too."

"That's right. Antimacassars. Old-fashioned things, but I can't bring myself to get rid of them. Now, you sit down there, and keep your pen off the chair. I miss your gran, you know. I dare say you miss her, too. We used to take you out when you were little, you know. We used to go pushing you in your pushchair, right up the path to Highcliffe."

Matt nodded his head, but the strange feelings of loss and comfort that the smell of lavender wax brought to him couldn't be put into words.

"Well. What's all this about schools, then?"

Matt opened his notebook and read out loud, frowning at his own writing. "In what year did you first attend school?"

"Oh, lor'. Now you're asking. I was born in 1917, in the First World War, like I said. Should be easy to work out, but I can't say as I remember how old I was for school. I think I must have been about five. I remember the actual day because I wore some terrible black stockings that my mother had knitted for me and I nearly passed out from the itching and trying not to scratch."

Matt twiddled his pen and chewed the end of it. This wasn't going to be easy.

"I've got to ask you what clothes you wore, but that's question five."

"Huh. Once you've got me going, you'll find I'm hard to stop. You'll have to shout at me and get me sorted out. Let's do it properly then. Put down that I started school in 1922; it's near enough, and I can't think who could contradict me."

Glad to be getting on with it, Matt began writing the information down. Florrie tried to answer each question as he asked it, and they moved down the list in a businesslike way. Gradually, Matt became aware of something strange happening. A picture began to build itself up in his mind. A picture of a nosy, talkative little kid in a long school tunic, tied at the waist, and heavy lace-up shoes. The little kid loved to be in school, even though the school was very strict and there seemed to be a lot of copying work to do. She sat at a wooden desk, with inkwells that she had to dip her pen into, though she dreaded making blots, for she'd be hit on the hand with a ruler if that happened.

"Didn't you have detention, or something like that?"

"We had to write lines. That was one of the regular punishments, but what we dreaded most was the cane."

"Did it really hurt?"

"Miss Swift's did. 'Swift by name, and swift with the cane,' that's what we said."

But Matt discovered that there had been things that were worse than the cane. One time there had been a nasty illness, called diphtheria, spreading itself around in the school. It began with a sore throat that got very bad. Eight children had all been sent off to Freebrough Infirmary, and one after another they'd all died. The school had been closed down while all the walls and floors were scrubbed with disinfectant. Florrie had got a sore throat, and was sure that she would be taken off to the hospital, but hers turned out to be a bad cold.

"It sounds horrible at your school. I can't understand why you didn't hate it," said Matt, vaguely aware that he was asking his own questions now, and wanting to ask more, even though he'd got to the end of the history teacher's list.

"Oh no, I loved it. Loved every minute of it. You see, it was such an escape."

"An escape? What were you escaping from?"

Florrie pulled a long face and shrugged her shoulders. "From boredom, really. The endless boredom of being at home. You see, my father owned a large draper's shop. That was nearly respectable, but not quite. My mother was a very ladylike person. You know the sort: spoke beautifully, always worrying about correct manners and knowing the right people. She spent most of her life doing dainty embroidery. This room is full of it—the antimacassars, and the tablecloth, and that picture up there."

Matt looked up at a picture in a large, fancy golden frame. It was the kind of picture you see in churches. Men with beards, in long robes, standing by a well, and a woman in a long blue dress, carrying a big vase. What was so surprising was that when Matt got up and went to have a close look, he could see that the whole picture was made of tiny, neat stitches.

"I thought it was painted," he said. "It must have taken years and years."

"It did," Florrie said. "You see, the trouble was, I was supposed to be like her, all ladylike and sweet, and I couldn't do it. I couldn't do it at all. I was a disgrace, so they said. I enjoyed going to school because I could run and skip and do PE—drill, we called it then. I loved the lessons—history, English, geography. Finding out about things, that's what I wanted."

Matt shook his head. He thought she was crazy.

"I knew your gran at school, of course. We were the same age, and we were good friends, right from the start. Got some photographs of her, if you want to see. Haven't had them out for years. You get them. Yes, in that cupboard there."

The cupboard door opened with a squeak, and Matt sniffed at a different smell. Tea bags, he thought, and some kind of flowery smell.

"There," said Florrie. "That box. No, not that coronation

27

tin. Don't touch that. It's the box I want. Pull it forward. That's right."

The box slid to the front as though it was on wheels, but Matt found it quite heavy to pick up.

"Careful with it. Put it here on the table. Ebony this is, quite valuable. Look at the inside of the lid, lined with velvet, and this is mother-of-pearl round the edge." She ran her finger round a thin rim that shimmered with colors. The photographs near the top were quite modern and not very interesting, though Matt picked out one of his gran, just as he remembered her. Florrie thrust her hands down to the bottom, spilling photographs over the table.

Matt giggled. "They're going everywhere."

"Who cares. You can pick them up. Here's one. Look, here's Joyce and me about . . . oh, ten, I should think. Now here's a good one. Our school outing. Now you can see the dreadful tunics that we wore."

"Which is you?"

"Guess. I'm the one that's different."

Matt frowned at the rows of solemn faces, then pointed to one girl with a sharp, cheerful face and masses of long, curling hair.

"Correct." Florrie grinned with satisfaction.

"But why? Why are you the only one? All the others have short hair and fringes cut straight across."

"Huh. You may well ask. That was the fashion, you see, but I wasn't allowed fashion. I had to have my hair curled up in rags every night. Now, look here. Who's this?" Florrie held up another photograph.

"It's . . . it's my gran, and you, and your hair is short. They let you, after all."

"I cut it myself. Shortest hair in school I had. Well, I got

Joyce to do it round the back. Look at us, arm in arm, clinging like limpets. She was very shy, your gran; I used to lead her into trouble, but I used to look out for her. She changed, though. Later on, when we were adults, she used to look after me. Helped me out when I really disgraced myself."

Matt dug down to the bottom of the box and pulled up more photographs, more school outings, Sunday-school outings, weddings, and portraits. Then he caught hold of something hard at the bottom of the box. It was a small, framed photograph of a baby. The picture was brown and faded, but the frame was shining silver, with a pattern of curling leaves.

He dusted a bit of fluff from the glass and examined the photograph. A fat-cheeked baby with an embroidered, brimmed hat and a fancy coat. Florrie watched him in silence.

"This frame is really good," he said. "This is even better than the ones you've got on your mantelpiece."

Florrie still didn't speak.

"You should put this up there. You should have it on show."

She took the picture from him and looked at it for a moment or two. Then she smiled.

"Yes. You're right, lad. I should."

She got to her feet and put the photograph right in the middle of the mantelpiece. Her hand was still on it when the doorbell rang.

Matt jumped.

"This'll be her. Miss Mind-your-manners Mawson."

Matt giggled. "I'd better go."

Florrie picked up the baby picture from the mantelpiece and looked as though she was going to pack it away, back in the box. But then she stopped, and looked at Matt.

"No. You were right, lad. Damn respectability."

She put it back in the place of honor on the mantelpiece.

CHAPTER 4

A cold, strong wind blew over the hollow, and Matt snuggled further down into it, sticking just the top of his head out so that he would see the vans coming. He picked at the rough grass that grew on the sides and pulled it through his fingers.

That Florrie . . . she was telling lies, he thought. He knew that adults did tell lies, even though they always went on about it to kids as though it was the worst thing you could do. He knew that his mother lied sometimes, but she did it in a gentle, kindly sort of way. It was usually so that people's feelings weren't hurt. Perhaps it was more that she didn't quite tell the truth sometimes.

But Florrie had lied straight out. She hadn't been bothered that he would know, and she'd lied to Miss Mawson, who was a church person. Matt grinned to himself. Mind you, she deserved lying to, did that Miss Mawson. He hadn't liked her from the start. First of all she'd stared at him like mad, then she'd started on in a ridiculous voice about how lovely it was for Florrie to have a young gentleman visitor.

She'd wanted to know what he was up to. Wanted to know what he was doing at Florrie's house, but neither he nor

Florrie had explained. It was like they had a sort of unspoken agreement about it. Then Miss Mawson had ignored him and started talking to Florrie in a way that had made Matt go hot with embarrassment.

"And how are we feeling today, then, dear? Are we looking after ourselves, then?"

Matt had thought it sounded as though Florrie was a little child. It was the way people talked to toddlers. The thing that had really shaken him, though, was the way Florrie had answered, and that was when she'd lied, too.

"Poorly," Florrie had said, pulling a miserable, sulky face. Matt had never seen her like that. She'd been bossy and awkward, she'd been funny and sad . . . but never sulky.

"Poorly, I'm quite poorly. My back, you know, and my legs." Florrie had shaken her head and looked sorry for herself in a way that quite shocked him. He'd felt very uncomfortable having to watch her and had edged his way toward the door, saying that his mother would be expecting him back. He set off down the street, but then he'd passed his own house and come down to his secret hiding place near the pier.

He shook his head, thinking about it all. Perhaps Florrie was a bit batty; that could explain it. What was all that about the baby picture—putting it up, then taking it down, then putting it up again? Batty. Yes. She must be. Then he heard the sound of the vans coming, winding their way down the steep cliff road, and he forgot about Florrie and settled to watch the surfers.

They arrived in twos and threes, but soon they seemed to be everywhere. They came from the villages as well as from Seaburn Bay. Some of them were young men who hadn't got jobs, but they got together the money for the surfboards and the suits by saving and scraping and doing odd jobs. Matt stuck his arms up over the edge of the hollow and settled himself with his chin on his hands. The very sight of them made his body zing with energy. He longed to join them and go riding over the waves.

They were not like his dad, all worried about money for food and clothes and mortgages. They were the ones that refused to go trailing off to London, taking any rotten job. They came down every day to the rough gray sea, ignoring the bitter wind and rain.

A black van with a smart surfboard strapped onto the roof drew up. Matt craned his neck. Yes, he was right: Wayne Smithson climbed out of the passenger seat and ran round to his older brother, who was getting out of the driver's side. They both went to the back of the van and started lifting down the gear. Another van came alongside and blocked Matt's view. That was Jennifer Stonehouse's brother. It wasn't fair. He wished he had an older brother; that would sort out all his problems.

There was a lot of shouting going on down there, and Matt suddenly saw Wayne come out from behind the van and leap onto the railings that divided the bottom prom from the beach. He wobbled along for a few paces, then thudded down to the ground in front of his brother.

Matt pulled himself up, out of the hollow. He could do it now. He'd never have a better chance. He could go down and give Wayne a whack on the back, and he'd be in. Wayne would be sure to give him a good thump back, but so what? Matt would be down there, down on the prom with the surfing gang.

He crept forward, his knees still bent, slithering a bit on the wind-flattened grass. Then he stopped. Wayne was suddenly the center of a laughing group of lads. He was bent double, his hand to his back. He staggered along, then turned, his head nodding up and down. Suddenly Matt understood. He grinned. That was it. Wayne had been sent to talk to that old fella who was bent double and walked with a stick. Now he was telling his brother and his mates all about it. It was quite a performance, and Wayne had them laughing like mad.

Matt slid forward again. He could do that. He could burst into that laughing group and tell them about Florrie. He could make fun of her and imitate the way she'd walked when her back had been bad. He could copy the way her fat backside wobbled as she moved. He could show them the stupid way that she would suddenly say something loud. He could . . . he could tell them how she'd put that picture up on the shelf, then taken it down. He could tell them how she'd lied.

He stopped. No. No, he couldn't. He saw her again, dithering between the box and the mantelpiece. He saw her staring defiantly at him, and lying to that horrible Miss Mawson. No, he couldn't tell that. He couldn't tell them anything. He turned around and grabbed at handfuls of grass to pull himself up the bank.

"Damn," he said. "Damn, damn, damn it."

The surfers were going down onto the beach now; Wayne's brief moment as a comedian was over. Matt climbed back fast, back up to the top prom, suddenly anxious to get there without being seen. He was red-faced and sweating, and felt sick in his stomach. Sick with himself. He'd blown it again. He'd never get another chance like that.

"An excellent piece of work. Good detail. Carefully done."

Jennifer Stonehouse turned her glinting glasses toward Matt and nudged his elbow.

33

Matt jumped. The whole of the front row had turned round to stare at him.

"What? Sorry, miss."

"Don't be sorry, Matthew," Mrs. Teesdale said. "Just give me more work like that. If you go on producing work of this standard, I'll be recommending that you start the history GCSE course the year after next."

"What?" Matt whispered.

"Nerd," hissed Wayne.

Matt looked at Jennifer in desperation. "What was it she said?"

"An excellent piece of work," Jennifer repeated, waggling her bushy eyebrows at him.

"Urgh . . . give over. It makes me feel sick when you do that."

Matt sat through the rest of the history lesson in a daze. He couldn't remember ever being told that anything he'd done was excellent. He'd never cared, or thought that it mattered. It didn't matter now . . . not really, but he couldn't seem to stop a slight, self-satisfied grin from touching the corner of his mouth.

Fancy that, he thought. Fancy. Old Florrie did me a bit of good after all. Suddenly it filtered through to him that the lesson was coming to an end. They were all packing their history notes away. Matt looked at his empty page, then across at Jennifer's neat rows of writing.

"I hope this next piece of work will be as good as the last, Matthew," Mrs. Teesdale said as she left the room.

Matt grabbed at Jennifer Stonehouse's back and found himself clutching a handful of brown hair. He stared down at his hand, surprised at the silky feel of it on his skin as it slipped through his fingers.

"You get off," Jennifer snarled at him.

"No. Sorry. I just wanted—"

She turned round and punched him on the shoulder. "What's up?"

"What am I supposed to do?"

"Oh. Homework. I knew you weren't listening. You were grinning in a daft way."

Matt sighed and stared at the floor. Was she going to tell him or not? Why did girls have to mess around like this?

"She said you have to go and ask all about Seaburn Bay."

"Ask? You mean ask all that again?"

"You have to ask what Seaburn Bay was like before the war."

"Oh no. What about the questions?"

"Make up your own. We all have to make our own up this time. Thicko. You have to ask about the buildings and the shops and all the seaside stuff. You know."

"Oh, crikey."

"Let's have another excellent piece of work, Matthew." The eyebrows waggled again, and she went.

"Oh, hell," said Matt.

Matt followed Wayne Smithson up High Street. He walked behind him, racking his brains. How could he put it? What could he say? Wayne was his best bet: Wayne could get him in with the surfers. He often went down there with his brother. Matt had never actually seen him go into the sea, but then, that wasn't the point. It was just to be there. To hang around the vans and tea wagon and chip stall. To lean over the rails of the pier and shout to them.

He closed the gap between himself and Wayne, but he still couldn't think quite how to put it.

Wayne turned round, aware that someone was breathing down his neck.

"Sod off, swot brains," he yelled.

"Sod off, yourself," said Matt, and turned quickly down Silver Street. He was halfway along Silver Street before he slowed down. He was furious with himself. He'd done it again. Blown it.

His mother was chopping vegetables at the kitchen table. Somehow the way she was absorbed in her task and the thought of her serving up the dinner, all smiling and pleasant to the guests, seemed to fire his anger even more. He dropped his jacket on the floor and threw his schoolbag down on the table, knocking over a colander of cut green beans.

"Matt!" His mother's voice shrieked.

"Ma-att." He made his voice rise in a sneering imitation of hers, then headed toward the stairs.

"You come back here. You come back here this minute."

Matt stopped halfway up the stairs and sighed.

"You get yourself down those stairs and come back here."

Matt sighed noisily again and followed his mother back into the kitchen.

"Sor-ry." He sang it, the fury still burning inside him.

His mother raised her hand as though to slap his face.

"Go on. Beat me up. Hit me, then. My real mother wouldn't do that."

She dropped her hand, but the anger blazed brighter than ever, her face all red and her eyes full of tears.

"Don't you give me that!" She was shouting now. "I'm

36

your real mother, all right. I'm the one you were given to. I'm the one who feeds you and mends your clothes and puts up with your damn cheek."

"Your guests'll hear, shouting like that."

His mother pushed him inside the kitchen and closed the door, calmer, but still annoyed.

"I won't have it," she said. "I just want you to come in and behave in a decent manner. Hang up your coat and put your bag away. Do it. Do it now."

Matt went to pick up his coat, and his mother returned to her vegetables, chopping away fiercely at them.

There was a thud as the front door slammed. Matt and his mother looked at each other. It wasn't the usual polite entrance that the elderly ladies made.

Matt opened the door to the hallway. His mouth dropped open.

"Dad."

Matt's father came into the kitchen, not smiling, avoiding his wife's eyes. He went and stood in front of the fire with his back to it. He didn't take his coat off.

"Hey, Dad!" Matt hurled himself at his father, who grinned and gasped with the impact.

"Now then, Matt. Let's have a look at you."

"I thought you weren't back for another week."

"No." The muscles in his father's cheek tightened. "No, I wasn't. You see. . . ." He spoke slowly, searching for the words. Matt's mother had stopped chopping carrots and waited tensely for her husband to speak.

"I've walked out."

"Walked out? From your job?"

"Aye."

"Hooray!" Matt yelled it as loudly as he could.

His dad clapped his arm around Matt's shoulders. "Well . . . someone's glad, at any rate."

"He doesn't know. He doesn't know what it means." Matt's mother picked up the knife and started chopping at the vegetables, making a louder noise than ever.

CHAPTER 5

Matt stared at his empty cereal bowl. He'd been delighted when his dad had come back last night, and he couldn't understand why his mother had been angry. Now it had all changed around. His mother had gotten up seeming quite cheerful, and offered to take his dad's breakfast up to him. But then his dad had leaped out of bed in a really bad mood, saying that there was no way that he was going to start all that. He'd dressed himself at the speed of light, and sat silently through breakfast. Matt's dad was never one for talking a lot—he was a quiet man—but this was a different sort of quiet, and Matt didn't like it.

"Hey, Dad."

"Umm."

"Hey, Dad. 'Boro's playing at home next Saturday."

"Yeah."

"I thought . . . well, now you're back, we can go again."

His dad sighed. "There's going to be no money for football matches, Matt. Not unless I can find something else."

Matt tried again. "Well, not every week. I don't mean that."

"Not any week at this rate, lad. And I'm going to have to sell that poor old thing outside on the road."

"What? Not the van?"

"Aye. I'll not get more than a few pounds, though."

Matt thought hard, frowning.

"Well, if you'll not get much for it, can't we just keep it?"

"No, we can't," his father snapped.

There was silence between them, and they listened to the clatter of pans and plates coming from the kitchen.

Then his father spoke again. Kinder. Trying to explain. "There's the road tax, and the insurance, and petrol going up again. It's not just keeping it. It's the running of it."

Matt nodded, and got himself off to school as soon as possible. Even the thought of school didn't seem so bad after the tense atmosphere at home.

Florrie stood in front of the mirror in her hallway. She finished combing her hair smoothly into place, and then pulled a black velvet hat with a sparkly brooch down over her ears, tipping it slightly to one side.

"Mmm." She grunted approval at her reflection.

She put her coat on and fastened it.

"Right. This time you are going to do it. Get on with it, then."

She stretched up her hand to unfasten the bolt, then stopped.

"Yes. Might help."

She turned to the umbrella stand and pulled out a walking stick. She held the smooth wooden handle and prodded it on her polished tile floor.

"Umm. Might do some good."

She leaned the stick up against the stand while she undid the bolts. Then she picked it up again, pausing with her hand on the door handle.

"Right. Now. Stupid woman."

She pulled the door open till it stuck in the usual place, then she gave a great tug and opened it wide. She stepped down into the porch. Tiny beads of sweat appeared on her face, and her breathing grew harsh and fast. She planted her feet firmly on the doormat and propped herself up with the stick. But then her hands began to tremble violently, setting the stick wobbling, until she tossed it aside, where it clattered into the corner of the porch.

"Damn thing. Better without it."

She stood on the doorstep, bag in one hand, hanging onto the door frame with the other.

"Now. Calm down. Breathe deep and slow. That's it. There."

She put one foot outside, into the deep, rutted holes in her pathway. Her foot slipped.

"Oh, no. Please, no."

Matt stopped by the gate. He hadn't exactly been coming to see Florrie, but he knew that he would have to call again sometime to get his homework done. And, at the same time, he wasn't quite sure how things would be at home, and he could put off finding out for a while if he called in at Florrie's first. Then, as he got near to her gate, he saw that she was coming out.

Aha, he thought. Sneaking off to the shops while Miss Mawson's not around.

He reached the gate and stopped. He saw that Florrie wasn't going anywhere. She was white and trembly and she seemed to be stuck, with one foot in the porch, and the other skidding around in the holes in her path. He couldn't leave her there like that, but he also couldn't stop himself from glancing up the road to see if Wayne Smithson was anywhere in sight.

Florrie was whispering something faintly, over and over again. "Oh, please. Oh, please."

Matt went through the gate and put his hand on her elbow. He got the idea that it was only then, at his touch, that she realized he was there.

"Get me back in," she said.

He took hold of her arm with both his hands and heaved her in through the porch and back inside the house.

She clutched onto the bottom of the staircase, hiding her face in her arms, while Matt stood there, feeling awkward and wondering if he should just quietly go.

But then Florrie raised her head, took off her hat, and brought out a lavender-smelling handkerchief, which she used to mop her face.

"I bet you think I've gone mad."

Matt raised his shoulders and grinned. She sounded very much her usual self again. He remembered the last time that he'd been here, and all that fuss she'd made telling Miss Mawson that she was still poorly.

"You didn't really tell a lie, did you? You're not quite better, are you?"

Oh, Miss Mawson. I knew you'd noticed that. Well, I didn't quite tell her the truth, either. My back's better. My back's fine. I just seem to have lost my nerve. I'm not letting her know what's going on; she'll have me in one of those hospitals. Never liked the woman, but I need her, see. Need her to get my shopping done for me, just until I get myself properly sorted out."

Florrie moved easily down the passage toward the kitchen.

"I'm going to have a cup of tea, and so are you. You rescued me, you did. You have to have a cup of tea for that."

"Yes, sir." Matt saluted and obediently sat down at the kitchen table. He got out his notebook and pen. "I have to ask you more history questions."

"What? Whatever do they want to know all that for?"

"I don't know, but I got an 'excellent' last time."

"Oh, well, we'd better make sure you get an 'excellent' again."

As Florrie answered his questions, Matt began to see pictures of a very different Seaburn Bay. Different from the one he'd always known. He saw a busy, fashionable place, where rich people came to spend their summers. Where ladies in long expensive dresses and beads and fancy hats wandered through the Valley Gardens with men in smart suits and scarves. They spent a lot of time drinking cups of tea and dancing outdoors to the music of bands. They raced old-fashioned sports cars along the beach, and larked around in the sea wearing baggy swimming costumes with long legs and frills.

Funny wooden stages were set up in the gardens or on the promenades or even on the sands, where singers and dancers called pierrots did concerts.

The pierrots were young Florrie's favorites and, much to her parents' horror, she had made friends with the couple who ran the pierrot shows. Their pierrot names were Petronelli and Maria, although they came from Leeds and everyone called Maria Mrs. Pet. The Pets taught Florrie to sing all the popular songs of the time, until her mother discovered that she spent her Sunday afternoons with the pierrots instead of at the Sunday school. Then there was dreadful trouble.

"I still went to see them, though. Joyce, your gran, used to cover up for me, and sometimes we both went together. Even when I'd left school and was supposed to be helping my mother with the fiddly embroidery that she did, I used to sneak away, making any old excuse, and go running down the bank to see the pierrots. They had a wooden stage with a sort of hut built on it. It was down in the Gardens, close to the fountain. There were two big doors at the front that they opened up and folded back, like scenery. We youngsters could pay a penny to sit on benches at the front, and behind there were rows of deck chairs for the adults. They had to pay more, of course. People used to gather on the bankside, too. You didn't really have to pay if you sat there, you just had to dodge the bottlers when they came around."

"What's bottlers?"

"Young lads, part of the pierrots' troupe. They came round with a bottle, see. Shaking it and collecting money."

"It sounds like a good laugh. I wish we still had pierrots."

"Oh, so do I. They did give us a laugh, you're right. I loved the bit where they all used to stand around in a semicircle and take turns at singing a song or saying a rhyme. Then they'd all go:

> That was a cute little rhyme that was,
> Tell us another one, do.

"The next pierrot would step forward then, and do a turn, and off they'd go again:

> That was a cute little rhyme that was,
> Tell us another one, do.

44

"Sometimes they told us rude rhymes"—Florrie grinned as though she'd enjoyed the rude bits—"but they'd also sing the most romantic songs."

Florrie tipped back her head and waved her hand in time as she sang,

> " 'Red sails in the sunset, way out on the sea,
> Oh carry my loved one, home safely to me.' "

She sang it in a wavery voice, and her eyes went watery. Matt smiled at the thought of it all. He was glad that his gran and Florrie had had some fun in spite of all the rules and restrictions. Even though they'd gotten into trouble for sneaking off to the pierrot shows, he could tell from the way Florrie spoke that it had been worth every bit of it.

"When I was really little, there were the bathing machines. You'd have laughed if you'd seen them."

"Bathing machines?"

"Daft little huts on wheels, just like tiny caravans. The ladies got changed inside them, then they were wheeled out to sea in the huts so that they could paddle and swim without having to walk down the beach in their costumes with everyone looking at them. You should have seen the costumes, though: They covered their arms and legs like baggy pajamas. There was nothing to see. There was a long row of bathing machines all drawn up beside the pier. They were there right up until the war, though by then nobody used them any more."

"You mean where the surfers park their vans?"

"That's exactly right. Oh, lord. What the ladies would have thought of all that surfing, I don't know. Or what the surfing lads would think of those ladies, come to that."

"Yes. I watch the surfers. I wish I could do it; it'd be great."

"They're grand, aren't they? Believe you me, if I were young now. . . ."

Matt had done a lot of writing, without really noticing that he was doing it. He found himself telling Florrie about his dad coming back from London, too. It was getting quite late when he said that he'd have to get off for his tea. Florrie walked back to the door with him. He could see that she began to lose the color in her cheeks as he stepped out into the porch.

"Are you feeling poorly again?"

"It's more daft than poorly, though I've heard of it happening to people. It's the porch and the pathway. That's where I fell, when I hurt my back, and I just can't seem to get past it. I keep thinking I'm going to fall again."

"Yes," said Matt. "It's made you scared."

"That's it. If I could just get to the gate. That's what I think. If I could get myself to the gate, I'd be all right."

Matt jumped easily across the rutted pathway that was giving Florrie so much trouble.

She watched him from the hall, hesitating to close the door.

"Do you . . . do you think . . . ?"

He turned, not quite hearing what she was saying.

"Do you think you could just stand there for a moment, and let me try to get to the gate? I think I can do it better if somebody's there."

Matt stared and bit at his lip. He hoped she wasn't going to start falling down again.

"Go on, then."

Florrie moved forward, with a look of strong determination. She got across the doormat without trouble, but as she stepped down from the sill onto the cracked tarmac, her shoe slipped a bit, and Matt could hear her breathing fast and hard. He took a step toward her, but she firmly flipped her hand at him to shoo him away.

"Got to do it myself. No good letting people lead me around."

She took another step, but her heel skidded in the broken rubble. Matt saw that her face was wet with sweat, and her cheeks were white.

"Damn it," she whispered. "No damn good. Get me back in, lad."

Matt grabbed her elbow, the way he had before, and steered her back into the porch.

"It's not your fault," said Matt. "It's the path; it's rotten. I'm going to get my dad to come and mend it."

"It's me," Florrie insisted, "not the path. I'm such a fool."

"No. It's the path that's dangerous, and my dad will sort it all out."

CHAPTER 6

"It'll need completely new tarmac, or concrete, and that'll cost money. It's not that I mind doing it, Matt. It's just the money."

"But, Dad—"

"Eat your tea, Matt." His mother was unusually sharp.

He did as he was told, shoveling large forkfuls of mashed potato into his mouth, far too fast. Then he stopped, feeling as though he was going to choke. The grey-white lumps suddenly looked disgusting. He couldn't believe it. It just wasn't like his dad. His dad would do anything for anyone. He hadn't expected this, he'd just taken it for granted that his dad would help. It wasn't even as though he was angry, telling Matt that he shouldn't have gone offering things without asking first. He just couldn't be bothered. Matt had thought his dad would be straight off up the street, measuring Florrie's path, breaking up the old crumbling bits.

"She's been telling me all about Gran," said Matt. "How they were friends and how they tried to get each other out of trouble when they were young."

Neither of his parents answered. There was just the click

of the knives and forks, but Matt saw that his mother wasn't eating.

There were times during the next weekend when Matt found himself actually wishing that he was at school. His mother suddenly decided that it was necessary to clean out the whole house. She banged and crashed around, scrubbing and vacuuming, taking down curtains, moving furniture, and generally making every corner of the house thoroughly uncomfortable to be in. His dad was out most of the time, though Matt didn't know where he'd gone.

Matt went out with his skateboard and spent the afternoon banging down the street on it. He kicked it along faster and faster, shouting the worst words he could think of and giving the finger to anyone who complained or got in his way.

Why had his dad come home, if it was going to be like this? Having him far away in London was no worse than this. This was horrible. He'd be glad to get back to school on Monday, and that was really saying something.

He walked slowly down Silver Street on the Monday teatime. He didn't want to get home. He stopped outside Florrie's door and examined the path. It had great wells of worn, loose tarmac, with daisies and roots from an old lilac tree breaking through it. Fresh anger filled him as he kicked at the loosened lumps. He wasn't going to go home. Well, not straight away. He'd go and see Florrie instead. He didn't have any more history homework to do, but that didn't matter, he'd just go and see her anyway. It would be better than going home.

*   *   *

"Have you got a rake?" he asked.

"What do you want with a rake?"

"Well, I could get all the loose bits off your path. It would make it a bit better. A bit safer."

He didn't say that his dad wouldn't mend the path. He couldn't bring himself to say that.

Florrie frowned at him for a moment, but then went and opened the door to her cellar.

"You go down and see what you can find."

She didn't say anything about his dad, and Matt was grateful for that, but he could tell that she'd guessed what had happened all right.

"There. This'll do the job." He brought out a rusting hoe.

"If you're sure?"

"Yes. I can do that, it's easy."

Matt carried the hoe through the house and set to work on Florrie's path. He banged it up and down, loosening the crumbling bits, then scraped them all together in a pile, and shoveled the bits away into her bin. He worked hard at it, and Florrie watched him anxiously out of the window. By the time he'd finished, it looked a lot better. He couldn't get rid of the holes, but at least you could see clearly where they were, and all the chipped bits were gone.

She insisted that he have a cup of tea, but when he went to sit at the kitchen table, she tutted and fussed.

"No, no. You come and sit in the front room. You come and sit in the comfortable chair."

"What? The rose brocade?"

"Of course. Why ever not? You get yourself sat down."

Matt sank back into the soft pink material and sipped his tea. This was the best he'd felt all day. No, it was the best he'd felt since his dad had come home.

He looked up at the baby picture that was still enjoying the place of honor on the mantelpiece.

"It looks good there," he said. "Whose baby is it, anyway?"

Florrie picked up the picture, held it up close to her eyes. "He was mine," she said. "But he died."

"Oh," said Matt, horrified by the sadness in her voice. "That's awful."

"Yes. But it's all a long time ago now."

Matt sat comfortably in Florrie's front room for a long time, and it was Florrie who eventually suggested that he ought to go.

"They'll be wondering what's happened to you."

"Don't care much if they do, but s'pose I'd better go."

When they got to the doorway, Florrie admired the work that he'd done. Matt stopped on the doorstep.

"Try again," he said.

"What?"

"Try again. Try to get to the gate. I'll stay here. Like I did before."

"Oh, I can't. I just make a fool of myself."

"No. Go on. Try it again. Now the path's better."

"Oh, all right, all right. Bossy fellow you are."

Matt giggled. "Come on. I bet it'll be okay."

Florrie put one foot down from the doorstep. Matt knew from the way her hands clenched that it was hard for her, but she planted the other foot firmly down, and there was no slipping or skidding about.

She took great gulps of air, then she stood still. He thought she was stuck again, but then he saw that she was just keeping calm, sorting herself out. As she breathed out, her shoulders went down, and the hunched, tense look faded. Her fingers uncurled and she smiled.

"I'm going to do it," she said. She took another small step forward, and then another.

"You're nearly there," said Matt.

Another step, and she grabbed hold of the gatepost.

"I've done it," she said. "I've got here." Matt felt as though he ought to clap.

"Now, just stop there, lad. Can I get back again? That's the thing."

Matt held his breath, and she walked back to the porch, slow and careful. She turned around on her doorstep, grinning like mad. "Well, I'll be damned. Now you've really sorted me out. Next time, I'd like it if you'd walk down to the bottom of the street with me. We could go and watch the surfers down on the front. Now you get off home, before your ma gets the police out looking for you."

Florrie closed her door. Matt stood by her gate.

Next time? he thought. What was he doing? She was taking it for granted that there would be a next time. He wasn't sure. It'd been convenient to call this time, but he wasn't sure that he'd do it again.

Both his parents came into the hall the moment he opened the door.

"And before you start," he said, "I've been trying to sort out Florrie's path for her. Seeing as you wouldn't do owt."

The next day, as he came home from school, he saw that there was a piece of roughly torn cardboard propped up against Florrie's gate. He came closer and saw that it said

WET CONCRETE. The path was neat and smooth and mended. He grinned. Florrie's door was closed, and it wasn't Florrie that he wanted to see at that moment, it was his dad.

He ran down the street and through the house. His dad was out in the yard sawing wood. He knew. He knew just from the look of his dad's back and the purposeful sawing that things were somehow better.

"Dad! You did it. You mended Florrie's path. You've made it all smooth."

His father nodded, and shouted over the sound of the saw, "Aye. Got a bit of concrete left over from a job Fred Jenkins is on."

"It looks great," Matt shouted.

His father stopped and put down the saw.

"Aye, well, it'll do the job. I was thinking we might have a walk over the cliff tops. We've not done that for ages, have we?"

A cool wind came off the sea, blowing their hair straight back. Their jackets belled out behind them, flapping at the bottom. Matt would usually have complained at this stage, and grumbled that he wanted to be getting home to see what was on the telly, but not this time. This time he was happy, really happy to be up there on the cliff tops with his dad, taking in great lungfuls of North Sea air.

"This is it," his dad said. "This is what kept me going, Matt, down there in London. Thinking about this."

"What? A grand view of the steelworks?"

His dad laughed. "The sea and the cliffs and the air. Mind you, there's nowt wrong with steelworks, not the way I see it. It's how folk have earned their living, and it's touched the landscape and marked it. What's wrong with that?"

Matt shrugged his shoulders. He hadn't thought about it like that.

"Give me this any day, you can keep your pretty places. I'm glad we came up here."

"I wish you'd never gone to London in the first place. I never wanted you to go."

"I know you didn't, but I knew I could get work there."

"Did you earn much money, then?"

"I did. It's not that the pay's much better, though, it's just that there is the work. You can work all day and night. But then, of course, you've got to pay for your lodgings, and working at that rate . . . well, it starts to get you down."

"Was that what made you chuck it in, then?"

"That and other things. It wasn't just one thing that brought me back, it was everything. It's the way of living. Eating, sleeping, and working with the same gang of fellows. Sleeping in bunk beds, all cramped and crowded. Hearing the same voices in your ears and no escape from it."

"We slept in bunk beds when I went on that holiday with my old school. It was great."

He laughed. "Aye, well, maybe you'd like it. Maybe it's all right for a few days, but believe me, Matt, it's no holiday. And I felt . . . well, I felt as though I was too old for it all. Too old to be going on like that."

Matt stood still, listening quietly. He'd never heard his dad talking like this before. Well, not to him, anyway. Talking to him like he was another adult, one of his mates. He hated the picture that came into his mind, of his dad's digs and the endless hours of work, but it felt good to have his dad telling it all.

"Most of the other fellows were young lads, you see. That was half the trouble: I seemed to end up doing the work of the foreman, though I never got paid for it. Because I knew how to do it, I'd end up sorting them all out. I couldn't stand by and watch them doing botched work that would have to be done again. Then I'd find that the foreman was sitting in the pub, knowing that I'd tell 'em all what's what. That did it. That finished me off in the end."

Matt nodded his head. "You done right to come back, Dad."

"Lost a week's pay by doing it."

"You still done right."

"Well, it's going to be a hard winter with money, and I'm going to need you to be right grown-up about it. Fred Jenkins is taking me on for a few weeks, to finish this job he's on, but then . . . I don't know. It's going to be scraping and making do, now the summer visitors have finished. There'll not be fancy Christmas presents this year."

"I don't care, I won't grumble. And you're not old. Well, not for a dad. Now Florrie . . . she's old."

Walking back along the cliff tops, Matt told his dad about his visits to Florrie and the history project. His dad laughed and seemed to think it was a funny way of learning your history.

"Well, it all sounds a lot more interesting than it was in my day."

As they came to the top of the cliff path, Matt's father stopped and pointed to the row of tiny cottages with the pub at the end, sheltering beneath the towering cliffs on the far side of Seaburn Bay.

"You've put me in mind of something my gran used to tell

us about. She used to live in that end cottage, you know. She's been dead for years now, but she used to go on about smugglers."

"Smugglers? You mean there were real smugglers here in Seaburn Bay?"

"Oh, yes. According to my gran, they were all at it, especially down in the Old Row. She told me that they had a special crib with a false bottom, and they used to hide brandy and stuff underneath the baby."

"What? Your gran used to do it?"

"She said she used to have to sit by the baby and keep it quiet when the revenue men came round."

Matt was fascinated and appalled.

"Florrie's never said anything about smugglers living in Seaburn Bay. Would she be old enough to know all that?"

"Well now . . . I think she would, although I do seem to remember that Florrie's mother was a very ladylike person, you know, rather fussy and proper. Wouldn't want her daughter knowing about that sort of thing."

"Yes, she's told me all about her parents; they were real strict. Florrie didn't take much notice of them, though. Florrie knows all sorts of things she wasn't supposed to know."

CHAPTER 7

"Smugglers? Of course I know. Everybody in Seaburn knows about the smugglers."

"They don't. They don't know anything about smugglers at school. Well, I've never heard about it."

Florrie folded her arms. She had a determined look on her face, and Matt thought he caught a glimpse of the sulky-child look, the one that Miss Mawson got.

They both stared at the floor in silence.

Then Florrie unfolded her arms and grinned. "We're being silly," she said. "You want to hear about smugglers. I want to get myself down to the bottom of the street. You walk down the street with me, then we'll both come back here and have a cup of tea, and I'll go on about smugglers till you're sick of it."

Matt still stared at the floor. It sounded like a fair arrangement, but he hesitated.

"We could walk into town if you preferred it."

"Oh, no. Bottom of the street would be better," he said quickly. He shifted his weight and dug the toe of his shoe into her carpet.

"I need you to do it," she said. "If I ask any of my neighbors or the church folk or any other, well . . . adult, they won't just leave it at that. They'll fuss. They'll be wanting to know all my business. I want someone to walk down the road and ask me nowt."

Matt did understand. He knew that if he mentioned it to his mother, she'd witter on about it for ages.

"Okay then," he said. He'd just have to hope that none of his friends would be around.

It was a bit of a struggle getting Florrie out to the gate, though she said that it helped a lot having the path made so smooth and safe again. Once they were out on the pavement and off down the street, Florrie seemed to be all right. She walked slowly at first and kept in close to the garden walls, but then she picked up speed, and Matt realized that there wasn't anything dreadful or embarrassing about it. He'd been worried that she might clutch on to his arm, or even lean on him, and that they'd have to go at a snail's pace, but all of that was quite wrong. In fact, once she really got going, Matt found himself putting in the odd running step to keep up with her.

They got to the bottom and crossed the road, and went to the fence to watch the surfers. There weren't many people on the top prom, just a few with dogs, having a Sunday stroll. It was busy down by the pier, though. The sea was dotted with small figures, riding in on the waves.

Florrie sniffed at the breeze and smiled, reminding Matt of his dad.

"This is doing me a lot of good. There's nothing like the sea and the smell of salt to get you going again. I'm right pleased with myself, and I'm right pleased with you."

Matt grinned.

"Is the cliff lift working?"

"Yes," said Matt. "They always have it going on Sunday afternoons."

"Good," said Florrie. "I'm feeling grand. Come on, we're going down to the bottom prom. We can't see them properly at all from here."

"What?"

"We'll get a better view from the bottom. Come on, lad. You don't expect me to slide down the bank, do you?"

And she was off, marching toward the hut where you paid to go down in the cliff lift. One of the carriages was waiting empty at the top. Waiting to carry them smoothly down the bank onto the bottom prom.

Matt followed her, but his legs were stiff and his face hot. A horrible feeling of panic grew inside his head, but his body seemed to be automatically doing as it was told. Bossed around by a bossy old woman.

The man who worked the lift greeted Florrie as though she was a long-lost friend.

"It's grand to see you again."

"It's grand to be out in the fresh air again," she said, pushing Matt into the lift in front of her. "Sit on that side. You can see the tank filling up."

Matt did as he was told. He was glad to sit down, as his legs had turned wobbly. Without thinking, he turned his head to the window and obediently watched as the man filled the tank on the side of the carriage with water. A strange feeling of comfort and a hazy memory came back to him. He had always watched the tank being filled, ever since he could remember. Just as he watched it emptying at the bottom. The weight of the water took the carriage down the bank, pulling the other carriage up from the bottom so that they crossed each other halfway.

They rode steadily down the grassy hill, and it was over all too soon. He turned his head to see the tank emptying.

Florrie stood up, ready for the man at the bottom to open the sliding door. "Older than me this cliff lift is, and it still works like a dream. Aye . . . you always were fascinated with that tank."

The man at the bottom opened the sliding iron-trellised doors.

Florrie was up and off and halfway across the prom before she turned around and waved to Matt impatiently. "Come on, Matt. What are you waiting for?"

"Hey?" He stared after her. A peculiar feeling that this had all happened before came to him. He wondered if he could be dreaming. He pinched the skin on the back of his hand.

"Are you stopping here all day, then, lad?" The lift man at the bottom wasn't as friendly as the one at the top. It was no good. The spell of the bossy old woman still held Matt prisoner. He followed her slowly, his shoulders drooping, head down. This had to be the most embarrassing thing that had ever happened to him.

He didn't really look ahead properly, but he was aware that Florrie was marching toward the side of the pier where the surfers gathered. Moving pretty fast, too. Straight into the middle of them she went.

"Hey, it's Florrie."

"Look, it's Florrie from the chip shop. Look who's here."

"Haven't seen you for ages."

Matt looked up.

"Grand to see you, love. You've brought us a fine sunny afternoon."

Florrie had vanished into the middle of the gang. He could hear her, answering all their greetings. He stared. They all knew her. This had to be a dream—either that or he was going mad.

Someone pulled a folding chair out from one of the old chalets and passed it through the crowd.

"Now, where has that lad gone?" Matt heard her say.

The crowd parted and there, sitting at the front like a queen surrounded by her court, was Florrie, and beside her was Wayne Smithson, grinning like mad at Matt.

"Come on, Matt," he yelled. "Your auntie's looking for you."

Matt walked slowly toward the front, and people stood back to let him through.

"Come on, lad."

"Look, he's here, missus."

He stood by Florrie's chair. She put her arm around him, just for a moment. Wayne Smithson flicked his ear, making it sting. He didn't care a bit. . . .

"Now we've got a proper view," Florrie said.

Later that afternoon, they walked back up Silver Street together. Matt was quiet, with a big, satisfied grin on his face. He was still waiting to wake up, but he'd decided that this was a wonderful dream, so he'd just go along with it and enjoy it while it lasted.

Florrie walked back up the street, slower than she'd come down it.

"I'll be ready for a sit-down and a good cup of tea. Though I haven't enjoyed myself so much for years."

Matt stopped as she reached her gate. "How is it? How do they all know you?"

"Oh, well, it's my chip shop, you see. I used to have that fish-and-chips stall, down there on the far side of the pier, by the roundabouts. I gave it up, oh . . . about ten years since. Got too much for me eventually. Hard work it is. They all used to come to me for their chips . . . little lads they were then. Used to hang around for free scraps. That Martin Smithson, your friend's brother, right little terror he was, but I had a soft spot for him. Funny how they all remembered me."

"What was that Martin said about a baby? He said something about that baby you used to push around in a pushchair. Then you gave me a shove and Martin laughed."

"That was you, lad. I thought you'd realized. It was when you were a tiny thing. Your gran, she used to come down in the cliff lift, wheeling you in your buggy contraption, and then, when I'd packed up my stall in the afternoon, we'd go wheeling you up the prom. Miles and miles we used to walk, pushing you up and down. More fresh air you got than any baby I know. Then we'd take you back up the bank in the cliff lift, and we always held you up to see the water rushing out of the tank. You yelled your head off if we forgot to do that. 'Course you were so little, you wouldn't remember it all."

But Matt smiled at the picture that came into his head and, in a fuzzy, dreamlike way, he thought he could remember.

Florrie turned round on her doorstep, fishing the key out of her purse. She stared at the gate and almost dropped the key.

"Look at that," she said. "I've walked through that gate and up my path without noticing that I was even doing it."

"So you have," said Matt.

"I've had a right good afternoon," Florrie said. "I've achieved something today, I really have."

So have I, thought Matt, but he didn't say it.

"Now," said Florrie, opening her door. "Now for the smugglers."

"The smugglers?" Matt stared. How could he think about smugglers when he'd been down on the front with the surfing gang?

CHAPTER 8

Matt stood at the front of the classroom, leaning on the teacher's desk. The history group was silent.

"And the smuggling went on for years and years, but in the end the revenue men caught them on the beach. There was a big fight, and the chief of the smugglers got killed. There was blood all over the rocks and blood all over the sand."

"Well, Matt, that's been really interesting," said Mrs. Teesdale, coming forward to reclaim her place at the front.

Matt grinned, then suddenly lost his nerve and went to sit down. Wayne bashed him on the arm and made a thumbs-up sign.

"That was very exciting, Matt. I think that would come under the heading of folklore, rather than history, but it's all linked. The stories that people tell are all part of the history of a place."

At the end of the lesson Wayne came up to Matt and thumped him on the shoulder as he shoveled his books into his bag.

"Hey . . . it was good, that. Do you want to go down to

the front with me? Our Martin'll be there. He'll give us some money for chips."

Matt stared at him. This was it. He'd wanted this to happen for months, and suddenly it was easy.

"Well, are you coming then? You don't have to."

"Yeah. I'm coming."

They set off along High Street, but instead of turning left down one of the side streets to the top promenade, Wayne headed on toward the old Valley Gardens.

"Hey? Where you off to? This is quickest, down Silver Street."

"Yeah," Wayne agreed. "But I wanna see how far they've got with the tracks."

"What?"

"You know. The old miniature railway. There's this gang of daft old fellas. They're mending up the tracks. Gonna get it all going again."

Matt followed him across the road and through the Gardens that sloped steeply down to the river where it ran into the sea. Once they'd passed the neat lawns and paths, they reached the overgrown part that the Council had neglected. Wayne picked up a stick and bashed aside prickly gorse bushes where the trees grew thick around an old stone temple, with pillars and steps, all covered in graffiti.

"Seen that place?" said Wayne. "I go in there to have a smoke sometimes. You got any smokes?"

Matt shook his head.

Wayne shrugged his shoulders. "Oh, well. Come on, nearly at the track now."

He went ahead downhill, fast, and stopped when he

reached the path that ran alongside the river. A group of old men with spades and tools were busy working on the old miniature railway track. They were leveling the ground and laying down new wooden sleepers. Wayne ran up and dumped his bag down beside the men. One of them stopped his work and got slowly to his feet. He stretched to ease his back, but couldn't quite straighten himself.

"Now then. Come to check on progress again?"

"Yeah," said Wayne. "We're getting some chips down at the front."

Matt suddenly recognized the man. He was the one that Wayne had been sent to interview for the history project, but he somehow looked quite different in his dirty blue overalls and his face smeared with grease.

"This track's going to be good," said Matt. "I never knew."

"Aye. You wait, we'll get her going, and spruce her up, and there'll be folk queuing up here to ride on her again, just like they did when I was a lad. We'll plant up these flower beds and maybe we can get the fountain going, and then all we'll need is the pierrots, with their prancing and dancing, and it'll be grand."

"What?" said Matt. "The pierrots? Was it here that the pierrots used to sing and dance?"

"Over there." The man pointed. "Over there, on yonder bank."

Wayne started kicking at the old sleepers that were to be moved, and one of the men handed him a spade and showed him how to lift them properly.

Matt left them and wandered over to the grassy bankside where the pierrot stage had been. He climbed up the edge and galloped sideways, trying to get the feel of what it would have been like up there singing and dancing, with an audience crowding around you. Suddenly the ground beneath him seemed to give. He stopped and then jumped. The ground bounced. He jumped again, and landed heavily. This time there was a slight creaking sound, and his foot slipped down and caught. Matt bent down, pushing the grass and weeds aside. His foot was caught in a crack of old rotting wood. The pierrot stage. It was still there, hidden from sight by the growth of bracken and grass. It was rotten and falling apart, but it was there, and he must tell Florrie.

"What you doing up there?" Wayne had tired of helping with the tracks. "You coming to the front or not?"

Matt got down carefully. The pierrot stage wasn't for telling Wayne about. He'd bring Florrie down here to show her. He'd make it a surprise.

" 'Course I'm coming. I want to see them surfing."

"Come on, then. Our Martin might let you have a go with his board."

"Would he really?"

"He might."

They leaned on the railings that separated the beach from the bottom prom.

"Devil's toenail, hang five, hang ten, goofy foot," Wayne shouted, waving his arms at the surfers.

"Ey? What's that?"

"Surfin' talk, that."

"What's it mean?"

"Don't mean nothing. You just shout it out. Good, in't it?"

Matt was impressed. He was really getting somewhere now.

"Would your Martin really let me have a try?"

"Sure. Sure he will."

Martin looked Matt up and down.

"Are you that lad that Florrie knows?"

Matt nodded. "Me auntie—well, sort of."

"Got no wet suit to fit you. Have to strip off. Then run home after. Got a life jacket for you, though."

"Don't mind. There's a bit of sun."

Martin smiled. "Bit of sun don't help much when you get in there. You a good swimmer?"

"Yeah. Well . . . not bad."

"Not the best thing to start on, my board. Bit tricky for a beginner."

"I'd go careful. Not go too far out."

"Okay," Martin agreed. "Strip off then, lad."

Matt stripped down to his T-shirt and shorts. He was glad he'd put his surfing shorts on, though he knew that he really needed a wet suit to keep warm in the cold autumn sea.

Wayne kicked Matt's clothes into a heap underneath the pier. They'd be getting covered in sand, but Matt didn't care.

"Are you gonna do it?" he asked Wayne.

"Nah. Let you have a go this time."

The sea was colder than Matt could have believed. He gasped and shivered, snorting hard to stop himself from yelling as the freezing surf swirled round his knees. The surfboard seemed to have a life of its own when he actually got hold of it, slipping and wanting to jump out of his hands, all out of control. He gripped it hard and gritted his teeth, then ploughed through the icy water toward the waves, puffing and blowing like mad.

The first wave was a big one and it knocked the surfboard clean out of his hands, carrying it back to the shore. He had to go wading after it, shuddering and embarrassed, while Wayne hooted at him from the pier.

He tried again, better prepared this time for the enormous bashing that came with the wave, and he hung on tight, but both he and the board were carried back to the shingle and dumped there. Matt was left scrabbling shamefully among wet pebbles. Wayne yelled and laughed, pointing down at him from the pier railings.

"Wipeout!" he yelled. "Wipeout before he's even begun!"

Matt almost wished that he'd never started this lark. The sea was covered with lads, riding high or rushing past him out to the waves, gliding out effortlessly. Why was it only him who was wallowing helpless at the edge?

"Here, let me give you a bit of a hand." It was Martin. "You'll freeze before you've got that board out. Got to get beyond the breakers, see? Stay up here near the white waves, and keep away from that rip current where the stream runs into the sea. That'll carry you straight out, and you'll be off to Holland before you know."

He lifted the board up and laid it flat on the swinging shallow water.

"Yeah. Thanks."

Matt knew he'd never get the board past those waves without help. It was embarrassing, especially in front of Wayne, but perhaps if he took notice of Martin, he'd manage to get out there and do something at least. He followed him out to the first waves, and watched how he tackled them.

"There. Point the nose out to sea. If you put it sideways on the waves, it'll jump up and smash you in the face. Now, like this: As the wave comes, dip your board into it, put your weight on and sink it under the wave. They're strong, these waves. Have to be strong to carry you back. Not easy, getting through them. Not as easy as it looks."

Matt gripped the board as the next wave pounded toward him. It nearly rocked him off his feet. He was glad of Martin's help, steadying the board from behind and tilting the nose down at just the right angle. The wave swung over them as they pressed down, then bounced up. They'd made progress. Matt laughed, his cheeks and fingers tingling now, and his hair flapping and wet. He moved forward to meet the next wave, facing it with confidence.

He passed through it successfully, then turned, rather shaken to see that Martin had dropped back and was nodding encouragement. Matt had taken that wave without help.

Right, he thought. Right. This is it. He was out there at last where he'd wanted to be. One of the surfing gang, battling against the sea. He turned to look up at the pier, but Wayne had gotten bored and headed off toward the slot machines.

There was a lad moving doggedly through the waves ahead of Matt. A slight figure in a yellow wet suit. He can't be much older than me, thought Matt. He certainly isn't taller. I'll follow him, copy what he does. Get the idea. But as each icy wave came crashing toward him, and the cold seeped right through to his bones, Matt found it harder to keep his grip on the surfboard. His fingers grew numb, and he reckoned that he'd gone far enough out. Perhaps he could just hitch himself up onto the board, and hope that it would carry him back to the beach.

But just then the lad in front tossed his head back and a

thick, wet pigtail flopped heavily down the back of the wet suit.

"Flaming heck," whispered Matt.

A strong wave almost wrenched the board out of his hands. He had to turn and grab it fast, before he got a chance to look at the small figure in front again.

"Flaming heck. It's never her!"

Even though he could only see the back of her, he knew who it was. Jennifer Stonehouse. Her with the waggly eyebrows. There couldn't be another, not with that thick brown plait of hair; it was a bit old-fashioned these days.

Matt stared as she turned, concentrating on her board, not seeing him as she pointed its nose back toward the beach. She watched for the right moment as the wave came close, then pushed off, lying prone on the board.

Yeah, thought Matt. She's gonna ride back on her belly. But then, suddenly, in a fast, smooth movement a bit like the push-ups they had to do at school, she was up and standing on her board.

"Hey, you," she yelled as she saw Matt and recognized him. "Out my way!"

She sliced through the sea, high above him, soaking him with a plume of white spray.

Matt's mouth dropped open, then changed to a wide grin. Jennifer could do that. He could do it, too. Excitement rushed through him, fierce and warming. He looked for the next wave just as Jennifer had done, then he too was up on the board. He heaved himself up until he knelt on the board, then, gripping hard with his toes, he forced himself upward, flinging out his arms to help him balance. For one fabulous moment he stood. Then the board tipped, his feet skidded, and he fell, cracking his chin hard. There was blackness, gentle drifting, then Martin slapping his face, and Jennifer's voice sounding all squeaky and scared.

Matt was vaguely aware that he was being half carried, half dragged across the beach and up the steps, though his feet hardly touched the stone. He was thrust into the back of a van that smelt of rubber and petrol. His life jacket and T-shirt were pulled off. He was rubbed hard and fast with a towel, and his own warm, gritty jumper was put over his head, bringing sudden comfort, though he couldn't seem to stop his teeth chattering or manage to speak.

"Now," said Martin. "You'll do for the moment. Best run you home. Get you sorted out properly."

Jennifer put his trousers and shoes down beside him. "Here, you'll be needing these." Wayne stood behind her, staring and silent and looking disgusted at it all.

Damn it, thought Matt. I've messed it all up good and proper. Got to be driven home. Nearly knocked myself out, made a right fool of myself.

He didn't resist, just huddled gratefully in the warm, messy back of Martin's van and allowed himself to be driven home, with both Jennifer and Wayne giving contradictory instructions as to where he lived. Martin ignored them both and found his own way to Silver Street because, as he said, "It's somewhere near to Florrie's house."

Martin spoke quickly when Matt's mother opened the door and turned white.

"It's all right, missus. Nothing broken I'm sure. Just cracked his chin, and got wet and cold."

There was a lot of confusion then, as everyone talked at once, except Wayne, who hung back, dead quiet.

At last, when Matt's mother had gathered some idea of what had happened and Martin was about to leave, Matt managed to mumble his thanks.

"Feel stupid. Sorry."

"Don't be sorry. You had a grand try. Been saying to our Wayne that he ought to have a try. Need a wet suit next time, and you need a bigger, steadier board. Come on then, Jennifer, we'll go and get your things."

CHAPTER 9

"Then the board seemed to jump up and hit me, *splat*, right on me chin."

"Ey, dear lad. A right wallop it must have been to cause all that." Florrie put her finger up gently to touch the blue-and-gray swollen patches on Matt's chin. "Lucky not to have cracked your jaw, I should say."

Matt gingerly patted the side of his face, examining it carefully in the mirror above Florrie's mantelpiece.

"That's it. That's what they've been saying at school. Oh, they've all been on about it, looking at it and fussing."

"Aye, I bet they have." Florrie tried to hold back a smile.

"It's bad, you know. It hurts."

"I can see it does. Still, bet it's got you noticed, ey? Bet you've had all the girls oohing and aahing and feeling sorry for you."

Matt had to grin, too. It was true, what Florrie had said. He'd never had so much fuss made of him before, and he had to admit that he'd enjoyed it. Only Wayne hadn't joined in. Hadn't even spoken to him. Still, he didn't care about that. He didn't need Wayne any more. Not now that there was Jennifer.

Jennifer seemed to have taken him over. She'd described all that had happened in detail, and the best thing was that she'd made it all dramatic, and she hadn't missed out how he'd actually gotten up on the surfboard and stood. Just for a split second, but he'd done it, she'd told them all.

"His first time on a surfboard," she'd said, "and he's off hot doggin'."

"Well," said Florrie, bringing him out of his daydream, "when are you going to do it again?"

"Again?" Matt sighed. What kind of an old woman was she? She was supposed to tell you to be careful and cautious. Not, when are you going to do it again?

"You want to get going properly now. You mustn't stop. Not when you've just got started."

"Yeah. S'pose so, but . . . well. I need a wet suit. That's what Martin said. You really need a wet suit, or you just freeze, and you've no chance then."

"Um. Yes," Florrie agreed. "Cost money, they do. I dare say they cost quite a lot."

"Yeah. And I can't ask me dad."

"No, you can't. Difficult enough for him, just now."

"I know where there's one that'd fit me, but it's Jennifer Stonehouse's, and I can't ask her. Anyway, you really need your own surfboard, too. I know Martin would lend me his again, but he said it's best to have a beginner's board to get the hang of it."

"Wait a minute," said Florrie. "Can't you hire them? I'm sure I saw it on the van that parks down by the front. 'Surfboards and wet suits hired by the day'."

Matt shook his head.

"I don't know how much, but it's still money, and my mum and dad can't spare any just now."

"No," said Florrie, her face all pink and excited. "No, they can't, but I can."

"What?" Matt looked doubtful. Although Florrie kept her house all beautiful, and she always made herself look smart, there was something . . . something about the way she never wasted food, and the careful way she counted pennies out of her purse, that told him she wasn't rich.

"I don't know. Mam wouldn't think that was right."

"Your mam needn't know."

She's got a right sneaky side to her, thought Matt.

"Listen," said Florrie. "I haven't got a lot of money to spare. I'd buy you all the gear if I had. But I have got a bit to spend on enjoying myself, and that's what it would be. I'd get a right good day's entertainment. I'd come down and watch you doing it."

Matt still looked worried about it.

"Look here. If I was younger, I'd do it myself. I'd be off over those waves like that Jennifer, believe you me." Matt grinned. She would, too. "But I can't do it. I've got too old. So you do it for me. It'll be nearly as good as doing it myself."

He still hesitated because, although he hadn't said so, it wasn't just needing the gear that was putting him off; he wasn't sure whether he could really face those freezing, terrifying breakers again.

Florrie picked up the picture of the baby who had died. She held it carefully.

"You see . . . well, there's another thing. I'd like to have done things for him. Never could, though. Never got the chance. It'd make me happy to do some of those things for you instead."

There was silence between them for a moment while they both looked at the photograph.

"What was his name?"

"I called him William."

"Okay." Matt nodded. "If you really want to help me get surfing, that'd be great." Then he remembered the old pierrot stage down by the fountain. "There's something that I want to show you, anyway. A surprise for you. Something that everyone's forgotten about."

They made their plans to go the following Saturday. Matt told his mother that he was going off to Redcar to spend the day with some of his mates. He felt a bit rotten about that, and he also felt a bit bothered that his mother had only to walk down to the bottom of the road and look down the bank, and she might see him anyway. Still, Matt knew there was no choice about it. His mother would think it was terrible to accept money from Florrie. However hard-up they might be, and however much anyone might wish to help, his mother had her beliefs about being independent. His dad was busy for a few weeks, helping a builder who was an old mate. He took up every awkward scrap of work that he was offered, and he wouldn't be around to notice what Matt was up to.

Saturday was fine but windy, and as Matt traveled down in the cliff lift, with Florrie, he watched the wicked-looking, white-tipped waves anxiously. Florrie was excited and full of energy. He could see that what she'd said was true. She was going to get some fun out of all this, and a faint feeling of resentment touched him. It was all right for her; she didn't have to go charging into that freezing sea. She didn't actually have to do it.

He even worried about hiring the gear—whether they'd have the right size; how you explained what you wanted;

whether it might cost too much. He needn't have worried about that, though. Florrie took over and sorted it all out, and nattered on to the man while Matt struggled into his wet suit. At last he was ready to brave the waves.

There weren't too many people around, as it was still fairly early, and Matt was glad of that. The wet suit felt very strange and awkward at first. Although the first swish of water inside it was freezing, it soon warmed up, and there was none of that uncontrollable shivering. In fact, it was only when a sudden wash of cold water came in through the neck that he realized how warm it kept him. Matt began to enjoy himself. Florrie shouted encouragement from the pier and waved her arms around a lot. Martin and then Jennifer came down and they both bellowed instructions above the crashing of the sea.

"Flat on your belly first."

"Try it kneeling. Don't stand up yet."

"Practice paddling with your arms."

"Now! Push off now!"

Matt managed to clamber onto the surfboard and ride back, stretched out on his stomach. Martin told him that he was doing grand and that was the right way to get going.

"Can't run before you can walk, lad. Practice on dry land, that's the best thing," he laughed, and clapped Matt on the back.

"What?" Matt was horrified. Waste time practicing on dry land! He wanted to go flying over the waves like Martin and Jennifer, and Jennifer's older brother, but to get up on his feet again seemed impossible.

Florrie went and got two lots of fish and chips from the stall that used to be her own. Betty, the woman who ran it, knew Florrie well. She'd been the young girl who'd helped when Florrie had been in charge all those years ago. She refused to take any money from Florrie now.

"There now," said Florrie, winking at Matt. "It's not working out expensive at all. We can do this again. You need lots of practice to get you going."

"I don't think I'll ever get up properly, though."

" 'Course you will. You listen to Martin. He says you're doing fine. He knows."

Matt went back to the sea for another session of struggling out against frantic waves that seemed determined to slap him in the face and steal his board. And although he enjoyed the fast ride back on his belly, and the wonderful sensation of the power beneath him, he couldn't achieve his goal. He began to feel exhausted with the effort of it all and the tension that seemed to come from the battle. He didn't want to give in and stop, because the gear had been hired for the day, and he wanted both him and Florrie to get their money's worth. When he looked back toward the prom he saw that Martin was bringing an old deck chair out of the back of his van and putting it up for Florrie.

Matt let the surfboard carry him back to the shore and he dragged it up the beach. Florrie had flopped back into the chair, looking washed out. He wasn't the only one exhausted with the day.

"Perhaps I should take it all back to the man," he suggested.

"Aye," Florrie agreed. "I think we've both done enough for one day."

"I was going to show you something, but perhaps. . . ."

"Oh, yes . . . the surprise. Well, where exactly is this surprise?"

"Round by the old dried-up fountain."

"What? Dried-up, is it? Well, I haven't been round there for years, and we don't have to go up the hill, do we? Go on, lad. I'm sure I can manage to walk round there, 'specially for a surprise. Now just fetch me a cup of tea from Betty's stall, and I'll be fit to get going again."

CHAPTER 10

The cup of tea revived Florrie, and she returned to her usual nosy, talkative self, having a long conversation with the men who were overhauling the track for the miniature train. Matt thought he'd never get her round to the overgrown bit near the fountain.

"Well, I shall have to go," she said at last. "This lad's getting fed up with me."

When they eventually reached the fountain, Florrie looked around, puzzled, wondering where the surprise was.

"Poor old thing," she said, patting the mossy stone side of the fountain. "We all used to meet here. It was quite famous, you know. Special mineral water. We used to bring little cups to drink from it. Supposed to do you good. Came from a natural spring. It was always busy, this bit. All the fashionable visitors promenading up and down, dressed up like I don't know what. Look at it now . . . old and crumbling and forgotten. Bit like me."

Matt frowned. She could really be irritating sometimes.

"You're not forgotten. Everyone knows you. There's Martin, Betty from the chip stall, the man on the cliff lift. Even the men who're mending the miniature railway tracks. It seems to me that everyone round here knows you."

"Huh. Take no notice of me, I'm a miserable old woman."

Matt ran over to the hidden, grass-covered stage. He jumped up onto it, and did his sideways gallop across it.

"Look," he shouted. "I'm on the pierrot stage."

"Oh, my goodness," said Florrie, and she sat down suddenly on the stone wall of the fountain.

"Look at me. La la la. Tra la la. You come up here and sing. Sing like you used to. Sing that song about red sails and the sunset."

Then he remembered how his foot had fallen through the crumbling wood, and he stopped and moved carefully to the edge.

Florrie for once seemed to be lost for words. He went back to her, suddenly sensing that something was wrong. Her eyes were full of tears. This surprise wasn't working out the way he'd hoped.

"I thought you'd like it. I thought you loved the pierrots."

Florrie nodded. "I did. Loved them more than anything. Still do. It's just that . . . it's a bit of a shock. And to think that it's been here all the time. I thought they would have pulled it down. I should have come to find out."

"Well, I expect the grass and weeds covered it over while the war was on. Nobody could have seen it after that."

"Yes. Yes, I'm sure you're right. The war stopped it all. The war stopped everything."

Matt scuffed the toes of his shoes against the side of the fountain. He was disappointed. He hadn't meant it to be like this.

Suddenly Florrie got up from the fountain, all agitated and

pink in the face. She turned her head from side to side, craning her neck, as though she was looking for something up among the trees. She set off, fast and determined, up toward the hillside where the plants had turned wild and woody.

"Where's it gone?" she demanded, sharp and angry. "It ought to be up here."

Matt ran after her. She made him feel worried and cross, carrying on like that.

"What?" he yelled. "What should be here?"

"Cupid's Temple, of course." She went scrambling up the bank, hauling herself up by grabbing at handfuls of grass and bushes, breathing harsh and fast. This odd behavior scared Matt; she'd never been quite as peculiar as this before. He was angry, too. She'd no right to go spoiling his surprise.

He caught up with her, and pushed in front of her, blocking the way.

"Stop it," he yelled. "Just stop it. I know where it is. I suppose it's that rotten old Greek temple that's all messed up. I'll show you if you stop for a minute. You stupid old woman, just stop!"

Florrie did stop. She stared at him. Her chin trembled as though she was going to cry. She didn't, though; she took a deep breath and seemed to calm down.

"Sorry. Don't know what I'm doing. So long since I've been here. Should have come before. Couldn't bear to come though, not at first."

"Didn't mean to shout at you."

"You did right. I needed shouting at. Show me where the temple is, and I'll behave decent . . . like I should."

Matt nodded and turned toward the thick bushes and ferns that hid the stone steps leading up to the Greek temple that was covered in graffiti. It was the place that Wayne used for his secret smoking sessions.

Florrie followed him calmly now. It was difficult going for her. Matt had to hold back branches and pull her up past bits that were muddy and steep, but when they reached the temple, she pushed past him and went to sit on the stone bench in the middle.

"Thank you, lad."

Matt stood still, watching her sitting there among all the rude words and disgusting drawings. She smiled up at him. It was a peaceful smile.

"I'm glad," she said. "Glad to be here, and I'm glad that you showed me the pierrot stage, too."

Matt nodded, satisfied. His surprise wasn't completely ruined.

"You see," said Florrie, "when I said that I loved the pierrots . . . well, there was one pierrot . . . they called him Francello. Well . . . I really loved him. He was my young man. But when the war started, the pierrot shows finished and he went off to be a soldier. He was killed."

"Oh." Matt began to see.

"He was . . . oh, very handsome. All the girls were after him. He had black curly hair and dark eyes, and they all thought that he was Italian; they didn't know that he came from Hull."

"Did . . . did you marry him, then?"

"No," she said, with a great sigh. "No, we never did get married. My father wouldn't hear of it. Francello was a showman. I was eighteen when he first came to Seaburn, and he joined the pierrots as a bottler. That just wasn't respectable. Father was horrified that I should go chasing after a bottler.

He didn't stay a bottler for long though, didn't Francello. He was so good-looking and he had such a lovely voice. That summer, the one before the war began, we were both twenty-one and he was the star of the show. We used to sit up here, him and me, up in this temple, looking down the valley so we could see when he was due to be on. Then he'd go sliding and slithering down the hill and I'd stay sitting here. His voice would carry, so I could hear him singing. Beautiful love songs they were."

Florrie sat there quietly for a while. Matt didn't want to disturb her, even though it began to get chilly and dark. He could tell that it was doing her good. She wasn't seeing the mess that the temple had become. She was seeing something else, from long ago.

At last she came back to the present, with a bit of a shake.

"Good grief, what are you letting me sit here for, lad? We'll both catch our deaths. Come on. It's back up in that cliff lift pretty quick. Time for another cup of tea."

Matt grinned. "You and your cups of tea."

They went back together in a comfortable quietness. Florrie was still thinking about the handsome young man.

When they got back, she made tea for them both, then went upstairs and came down carrying a faded brown photograph.

"I keep this separate," she said. "This is him. This is Francello."

Matt took the photograph. He saw a man with a scarf tied round his head, rather like a pirate, and dark, curling hair showing at the front. You could see that he wore makeup and had an earring in one ear. There was a frill around his neck, like the ones Punch and Judy wear, with two pom-poms down the front of his top.

"Yes," said Matt. "He looks great. I'd have thought he was a smuggler. I thought the smugglers looked like that."

Florrie laughed. "Oh, no. You couldn't tell a smuggler by looking at him. Smugglers wanted to keep quiet about what they did."

Matt got up and put the photograph on the mantelpiece. He propped it up next to the baby.

"You should have it up there," he said. "Sharing the place of honor with the baby."

Suddenly, he looked at the baby photograph, then the pierrot, and then back to Florrie.

"Was he . . . was the pierrot the baby's father?"

Florrie nodded.

"So . . . the man died . . . and the baby died, too."

"Well," said Florrie, her voice faint. "I didn't quite tell you the truth about that. I didn't know you so well then. You see, William didn't die. I gave him away."

"What? You mean . . . ?"

"Yes. I had him adopted."

There was silence while Matt looked again at the baby picture. Looked at it differently, with more interest.

"So he was adopted, too, like. . . ."

"Yes. Like you."

Matt frowned. "Why? Why did you do it?"

"It was the hardest thing I ever did, giving him up. You see, I had to leave . . . leave Seaburn. It was such a disgrace having a baby and not having a husband. My parents would have nothing to do with me."

"Where did you go?"

"I stayed with a vicar and his wife, who lived in the Dales, while I had the baby. They were people that your gran's mother knew. Joyce, your gran, was a real friend to me then. I wouldn't have got through it without her help. Well, the vicar and his wife knew a rather wealthy couple who hadn't been able to have any children, and they suggested that I should let them adopt William."

"But why couldn't you keep him?"

"I had no money, no job, and nowhere to live. I'd just heard that Francello had been killed. He died on the beach at Dunkirk. He was one of the ones they didn't manage to bring back. Well . . . I wanted my baby to have a father as well as a mother. I wanted him to have a better life than I could give him. I gave him up because I loved him."

"So you gave him to these rich people."

"No."

Matt frowned.

"Someone else had heard about me. People who knew me well, and knew Francello, too."

"Who were they?"

"Petronelli and Mrs. Pet."

"The pierrots."

"They'd had to give up the shows, of course, what with the war, and they'd moved to the south of England. They were running a small cinema and they had a house next door to it. They'd always wanted children, I knew that, but it had never happened for them. Mr. Petronelli had always been wonderful with kids, and I knew that they'd both adore William. So I gave him to them."

"Oh . . . I'm glad you chose them. Did you see him again?"

"No. Never. I thought it better like that. I thought having two mothers would be difficult for him. They sent me the photograph."

Florrie took the photograph from Matt.

"This photograph. It was very important. It's the clothes. I worked and worked to make him the most beautiful set of clothes. If my baby was to go to someone else, he wasn't going to go in rags. He was going to go looking like a little prince."

Matt looked again at the baby. "He does look like a prince," he said.

"Mrs. Pet sent me this photograph, and when I saw how she'd dressed him all up in the clothes that I made, then I knew. I knew I'd done the right thing and that they'd bring him up to feel proud of me. The clothes were so important, they meant everything."

Matt snatched the picture out of Florrie's hands and examined it again. His hands were shaking.

"What is it? What's wrong?" said Florrie, alarmed.

Matt thrust the picture back at her and ran out of the room. He went straight out of the house, down the road, in at his own front door. He pelted up the stairs, with his mother, shocked at the speed and the noise, calling after him.

He flung open the door of his bedroom and pulled out the bottom drawer of the chest of drawers. He started flinging things over the floor—a paint box, pencils, broken toys, odd socks—until at last he pulled from the back the thing he wanted. A white baby's jacket, crumpled and smudged with paint.

He held it up to the light and burst into tears.

"Matt. Whatever's wrong? What is it?" His mother stood in the doorway.

"It's dirty," he said. "I've got paint on it, and lumps of glue."

CHAPTER 11

Florrie stood by her front gate, clutching on to the gatepost and looking anxiously down the street toward Matt's house. She clicked her tongue, annoyed with herself.

"Now what have you done? Put your foot right in it, saying all that to a young lad."

She turned from the gate and went slowly back into her house. The baby photograph was lying on the chair where she'd dropped it. She bent to pick it up and carried it back to the mantelpiece. Then she took up the pierrot photograph in her other hand and held them together.

"Stupid old woman. That's what he said, didn't he? Stupid old woman, that's what you are. Should have kept quiet. Why go and say that, after all these years?"

She went over to her sideboard and opened the top drawer. She carefully put both photographs inside and closed it. She stood there for a moment, and then she pulled it open again.

"No," she said. "Stupid old woman or not. No going back now. No more pretending."

She lifted out the two photographs and set them side by side in front of the mirror.

Matt's father dumped his workbag down by the back door and went in. The kitchen was empty, but he heard raised voices coming from upstairs. He bent to unfasten his laces and slipped his shoes off before stepping out onto the hall carpet.

His wife clattered down the stairs fast, still shouting.

"What she thinks she's doing, I don't know. She's mad. She must be going senile."

"Linda, that you? What's up?"

She stopped, all red-cheeked and out of breath.

Matt followed his mother down the stairs, his face wet with tears, but he wasn't crying now; he was angry.

"Stop her, Dad. She's going to tell Florrie off. She'll spoil everything."

"What?"

"Tell her off! I'll do more than tell her off! Do you know that Florrie has been paying for him to go surfing? Paying for his wet suit and surfboard. Then she's gone telling him some story about her having had a baby and given it away to be adopted."

Matt's dad frowned, puzzled. "What? Florrie?"

"He's come in all upset. She's really upset him. I've never heard such rubbish. She's going to get a piece of my mind, all right."

Then there was a great slam, and she was off out of the front door, fast and furious, and marching up the street.

"Stop her, Dad," shouted Matt. "She'll spoil everything. Please, Dad. It's true what Florrie told me, and I *was* upset, but only for a minute. I like being with Florrie, and there's things . . . things I want to ask her. Run after her, Dad, and fetch Mum back."

"Well now, Matt . . ." His dad shook his head. "I don't know."

"Dad?"

Matt clung on to the bannister. He felt wretched. He wanted to go and shake his dad. Why did he just have to stand there in the hall with his hair full of plaster, looking puzzled and helpless. He's pathetic. He's just pathetic, Matt thought, then he thumped down the rest of the stairs and slammed out of the front door.

He chased up the street after his mother, shouting at her to stop, but she reached Florrie's house ahead of him, and he saw her give the doorbell a long firm ring. The door opened and he heard his mother's voice loud and angry.

"What on earth do you think you are up to? The boy's come home in tears. He's in a right state. Why go making up stories about you having a baby? Fancy upsetting him like that."

Matt reached Florrie's gatepost. He could see her face, pale in the light of the hallway, beyond the dark shape of his mother. Her chin trembled, but she answered calmly.

"It's not a story, Linda, it's true. I did have a baby that was adopted. I've never told anyone before. Your mother was the only one who knew."

There was a moment of stillness and silence, then Matt's mother stepped into Florrie's hall. She didn't see Matt hovering by the gate.

Matt walked slowly back to his own house. He avoided the front door and went to fetch his skateboard from the shed at the back, then he clattered and banged his way back up the street again, until he stopped level with Florrie's house.

There was no sign of life, no noise, no arguments or shouting. Then the light clicked on in the front room. He wished he could see what was going on in there. He wished he hadn't gone running home all upset in that daft way . . . it was just that it had caught him unprepared. It wasn't that he never thought about it. He did think about it. He'd always known that he'd been adopted; he couldn't remember a time when he didn't know. He'd often thought in a vague sort of way about his first mother, the one who he'd been born to. He knew a bit about her. His mum and dad had answered his questions, giving him the small bits of information that they had.

She'd lived in Freebrough. The name of the place was familiar because every morning, as he walked past the bus station, he saw the bus with *Freebrough* on the front. He'd never been there, though.

She'd been very young, still a schoolgirl, they'd said. His father had been a young man that she'd met on holiday. She'd never seen him again after their holiday romance. Matt'd had a dreamlike idea of a beautiful girl, like one of the older, most fancied girls in the sixth form at school, but suddenly Florrie had changed all that, when she'd started talking about the clothes that she'd made for her William. She'd made Matt think about the little jacket that his own first mother had sent for him. It wasn't a fancy jacket at all. It had mistakes in the stitches, and the knitting at the bottom was loose and wiggly, then awkwardly tight at the top. Matt had never taken much notice of it, and even thought of throwing it away, but his mother had insisted that it should be kept. He was glad that he had kept it now. He could see her differently because of it. A young girl who was no good at knitting had struggled to make something for the baby that she couldn't keep. It was something very precious, and he wished that he hadn't let it get so messed up.

Whatever was going on in Florrie's house was taking a long time. It was dark and getting cold, and he was vaguely aware that he was hungry. Matt crossed the road and dumped his skateboard in Florrie's garden. He put out a hand to the front door and found that it was open.

Huh . . . anyone could walk in.

He remembered the first time he'd come to her door. All the locks and bolts. He listened for the sound of raised voices, but could hear nothing. He pushed the door open and stepped into the hallway. Now he could hear voices, soft and low, coming from the front room.

They both looked up from the sofa as he walked in. They sat close together. His mother held the pierrot photograph and Florrie held the baby picture. They both smiled at him and giggled, almost as though they were embarrassed.

"Away in, lad. It's all right. Your mam's not played war with me. We've just been having a bit of a talk."

"I'm sorry, Matt," said his mother. "I shouldn't have seen red like that. I never knew, you see. My mother never told me about it, and when you came in, Matt, all upset like that, I was a bit shocked. I've known you all my life, haven't I, Florrie? You've been just like an auntie to me, and you don't think of things like that happening to your auntie. I thought you were going a bit crazy, and making it up, but I couldn't understand why. I feel very sorry. Sorry that you had all that trouble and sadness when you were young. I'm glad you've told me now. It's just that, well . . . I don't know how you must have felt when we adopted Matt. You were so good. You and Mum were such a help, and we were so worried."

"What?" Matt went to sit in the rose brocade chair. "Why were you so worried?"

"Well . . . there's always worrying. You are given this little baby to look after and you've wanted a baby so much, for a long time. You've gone around looking at ads for diapers and prams. Every time you open a magazine or switch on the telly, you see mothers and babies. Your friends all seem to be having babies, and you try hard not to be jealous. Your grandma and aunties drop heavy hints that it's time you had one, too, and all the time you want it to happen more than anything else, but it doesn't. You are a failure in the most terrible, secret way."

"Yes," said Florrie. "It must be rotten, feeling like that."

"Well, then you have the idea of adopting a baby, and it seems such a sensible way to sort things out. You need a baby, and a baby needs a home. You go off to the adoption society, thinking that soon all your troubles will be over, but of course it's not like that. There's long, grueling interviews, and there's more long waits in between. Even if you are lucky enough to get accepted, then you go onto another long waiting list."

"I never realized," said Matt. "I thought you just went along one day and got me. How long did you have to wait before you got me?"

"Well now . . . it took about a year and a half of interviews and visits, then we waited another two years once we'd been accepted as adoptive parents."

"Phew," Matt whistled.

"Then suddenly it happens. The phone rings, and you can't take in what they're saying. They tell you that there's a baby for you, and the next week it's there. You've got your heart's desire, and it's wanting feeding and changing, and keeping you awake at night."

Matt giggled.

"The social workers keep visiting you to see that you and the baby have settled down together. You feel as though you're on trial and that everything you do is being held up for inspection. They don't mean it to feel like that, but it does. Then you have to wait, maybe six months, maybe more, to make sure that the baby's first mother doesn't change her mind. It feels terrible because you want the baby . . . well, we wanted you . . . desperately, but at the same time, we would have understood if the mother wanted the baby back."

"Yeah," said Matt. "It'd only be fair."

"Then there was your dad's job."

"What had that got to do with it?"

"Well, first of all we had lots of long interviews to see if they thought we were decent and suitable to adopt a baby. At that time, your dad had a good job with Jenkins, but it was while we were waiting for the adoption to go through that Jenkins went bust. We were terrified that if the social workers found out that your dad was out of work, they might think we weren't suitable anymore."

"Would they really have changed their minds?"

"We were never sure, we were just worried sick about it. Your gran and Florrie were really good. Kept us going. Gran said that we could have her house, so that at least we'd always have a home. But what did you think, Florrie?" She turned anxiously toward her. "Didn't you start to think that perhaps we shouldn't have kept him, when we were so short of money?"

"Not a bit," said Florrie. "I thought you were fine parents for Matt, and I still think you are."

They all smiled, suddenly shy with each other.

"I tell you what sticks in my mind," said Florrie. "Do you

remember the night of the adoption? The evening when you'd been to court?"

"Oh, heavens, yes. That was so silly, wasn't it?"

"Ey?" said Matt. "What happened?"

"You tell him," said Florrie. "It wasn't silly, it was good. It was just right."

"Go on, Mam."

"Huh," his mother grinned. "It was stupid in a way. We'd had all that worry for such a while, and we'd hardly gone anywhere or done anything. You don't when you've got a baby to see to. Well, we decided that after we'd been to court and got it all sorted out, we'd have a celebration. Your gran and Florrie said that they'd baby-sit, and we were going to go out and have a smashing meal and go to a disco. Your gran was going to treat us."

"What? You and Dad, go to a disco?"

"Yes. We *were* capable, you know."

"Well . . . what happened then?"

"I don't really know. We went, and we had a nice meal, but suddenly it just all felt wrong. The music seemed horribly noisy and the lights too bright, and I suddenly got a dreadful feeling of sadness. We were so happy, but we were happy because someone else had felt they must give their baby to us."

Florrie pressed her hand, and Matt waited, all quiet.

"I burst into tears, and your dad took me home."

Matt frowned. "Sounds as if it was a right washout."

His mother smiled at Florrie. "It wasn't. When we got back, you'd woken up, and Mum was walking the floor with a screaming child. As soon as I came in, you stopped. That felt good. Then, because it was still early, Mum and Florrie stayed for a bit, and we all sat round together, the four of us, having a quiet drink and passing you from knee to knee, talking about the future and our plans. . . . That felt right. That was a celebration, and it was the right kind."

"It was a grand night," said Florrie. "Joyce and me, we couldn't help but laugh at them. We'd been itching to be baby-sitters and we thought we'd got our chance at last, but no . . . there they were, back again. You were a very much-wanted baby, my lad. You bear that in mind."

Matt grinned.

CHAPTER 12

Matt had a strange mixture of feelings as he and his mother walked down the street back to their house. The strongest thing was a comfortable closeness to his mother, but he couldn't ignore the touch of sadness that came from thinking about Florrie and her William, and about that young girl who'd knitted a tiny baby jacket for him.

"I tell you what, Matt," his mother said, as though she'd heard his thoughts. "I'm sure I could make that little jacket nice again. I've got some special stuff that you soak wool in. It brings it up lovely, all clean and soft. I'll do that, shall I?"

Matt nodded. "Yeah. I'd like that. I'll wrap it up this time, and I'll keep it nice."

That evening seemed to change things. It was almost as though, from then on, Florrie became part of Matt's family. His mother often sent him up the road to invite her to have Sunday lunch with them. It was rare that they could afford a proper roast, but they usually managed to make it a special meal, and Florrie brought down delicious homemade cakes. Matt's dad called in at Florrie's house and did small repair jobs for her. Matt often found him there, having cups of tea and talking about the dreadful shame of the Grand Hotel being left to crumble away on the seafront. They recalled the days when it was the finest hotel in the county of Cleveland and swarming with rich visitors. Florrie knew about Matthew Walker, who was Matt's father's dad. He had been one of the stonemasons who'd worked on the skillfully carved balconies that still stood solid and strong, refusing to let the years of neglect destroy them.

Matt's mother and Florrie sometimes went off to Middlesbrough on the bus when they had some special shopping to do. But more often they went round the jumble sales, looking for bargains. They would come back all excited, carrying big bags bulging with warm sweaters and decent curtains that might just fit, and odd flowered plates that they'd bought for a few pence. Half of the stuff was really useful and cleaned up well; the other half had to be taken back to the next jumble sale.

Florrie continued paying for Matt to hire a surfboard and wet suit, although it wasn't in secret anymore. Almost every Saturday, he was down at the front with the surfing gang, and Florrie usually joined them for a while, getting Matt free chips for his dinner. He gradually gained confidence in the water and he gritted his teeth and let Jennifer Stonehouse boss him about a bit, trying to help him and give advice.

There were times when he got fed up with it all because, despite everything, he still couldn't quite manage to stand on the board and go riding over the waves. But Florrie would not allow despair.

One Saturday afternoon, Matt came out of the sea and

flopped down on the bench by the pier, where Florrie was sitting with a rug over her knees. He was exhausted and miserable because he seemed to be getting nowhere.

"You've just got to get back in there and try again," she said. "Don't let the waves frighten you. They can knock you down, but they can't stop you getting up and trying again. Everything's like that, lad. It's what the whole of life is like. You mustn't ever give up. You have to sort yourself out, get yourself together, and start all over again."

Matt nodded in agreement, but it was easier said than done, and he knew that there was more behind Florrie's words than surfing. A disturbing sense of sadness caught in his throat. He turned to look at her sitting there on the bench, plump and solid, white hair blown back and her cheeks whipped pink by the wind coming straight off the sea.

"Is that what you did?" he asked.

She looked round at him sharply.

"I mean . . . after Francello had been killed, and William had been adopted. Did you have to start again then?"

"Oh yes, I had to start again. Mind you, I did what I'd always wanted to do; I joined the QAs."

"QAs?"

"Queen Alexandra's Nurses. I'd always wanted to train to be a nurse, but my parents didn't approve. Not ladylike enough. Can you imagine it: They called me Florence after Florence Nightingale, and then they objected to me being a nurse."

Matt laughed.

"So there you are. Some good came of it all. I did what I wanted to do. I went off to France after the D-day landings. I was one of a team of nurses who'd had special training. We'd been ready and waiting for weeks."

"Wasn't that exciting?"

"No, not exciting, terrible. It did me a lot of good, though. Made me realize that I was lucky just to be alive. But it wasn't only then. . . . I've gone on all through my life like that, starting again. There was the time I came back to Seaburn Bay. That was after my father had died. He never forgave me, but Mother did. After he died, Mother begged me to come back, so I did, and I looked after her till she died. Then there was more starting again to do. That was when your gran and me opened the tea shop. Goodness, how we worked at that! We had to do it all ourselves: decorating, cooking, serving, even made our own posters. Still, it was a grand time that, one of the best, and it worked—we made a go of it. Then later I went on to the fish-and-chips stall. More starting again. It's all good in its own way; you just have to keep at it, and never give up."

"Yes, suppose so. Might just have another go, before this suit has to go back."

"That's it," said Florrie. "You know, I think *you* got me started again, when you came knocking on my door with that horrible basket of fruit."

"Me? Got you started again?"

"Yes," she grinned. "Yes, you did. I wasn't doing too well, you know, what with that fall I had, and feeling a bit out of touch. Yes, I'd definitely say that you got me started again."

"Well," said Matt. "I'm glad if I did. And *you* got me going on this surfing all right. I'm off to have another go right now."

One evening, after Matt had spent the day fighting to stay on a surfboard, Florrie asked him to come back to her house.

"Got an idea," she said. "Something I want to show you. Want you to have it, actually."

Matt was intrigued. He followed her into her front room. The coronation tin was out on the table. Matt recognized it. He'd seen it before, when she'd showed him her photographs.

"Thought I wasn't supposed to touch that. Thought that was really special for some reason."

"It is special. Very special. Decided to open it, though."

She pulled off the lid. It was crammed with sealed envelopes.

"There's money in here," she said. "I want you to buy a surfboard with it."

Matt stared. "What! Where's it come from?"

"Me, of course. There's fifty pounds. One for every year of his life. Some of it will be old money—you can't spend that. We'd be able to sell it, though, to one of the coin dealers. Might be worth quite a lot, some of it."

Matt scratched his head. He still couldn't work it out.

"But. . . ."

"It's his birthday money, you see. Every year on the third of June, William's birthday, I bought him a card. Then I put one pound in it and sealed the envelope up, and I, well . . . just shoved it in this tin. At first I thought that perhaps I'd send it all to him, someday. It was really daft, but it made me feel better. It became a sort of ritual, a silly habit. But anyway, I want to give it to you now."

Matt's eyes filled with tears. He couldn't think of anything that seemed the right thing to say.

"I wouldn't want to give it to anyone, but I know I won't ever give it to William. I've got right fond of you, and with you being a young lad who was adopted, well . . . that makes it feel right."

She picked up the top envelope and began to open it, but Matt stopped her. He took it out of her hand and put it back in the box. Then he picked up the lid and pressed it down on the tin. "No. This is William's money. I won't take this. You can go on hiring the gear for me, but I won't have this."

Florrie looked disappointed at him, but he was firm.

"If," he said, hesitant now, "if I *were* William, I'd want you to use this money. I would want you to spend it on yourself."

Florrie shook her head. "No. Couldn't do that."

Matt took the tin and pushed it to the back of the cupboard where he knew she usually kept it.

Florrie sighed. "Well, if you won't have it now, I'm going to leave it to you in my will. You'll have it when I die."

Matt grinned. "Okay. Do that. You aren't going to die for ages yet."

"Not if I can help it," she agreed.

Matt had gone back to his house, torn between pleasure and distress. He could almost chuckle to himself at the kindness of her wanting to give it all to him, and yet the picture in his mind of lonely young Florrie buying cards that she would never send was almost too upsetting to think about.

There had been many questions that Matt had wanted to ask about William, and now he discovered that it was not difficult to ask after all. Florrie wanted to talk about her child, that was clear. She wanted to go over every detail in her mind: his dark, curly hair; the urgency of his cry in the night; the strength of his tiny, curled fingers; his fat, kicking legs.

One time she'd told how she'd asked Joyce to arrange for Mrs. Pet to come and take William, as she couldn't bring herself to do that bit. Joyce had worked it all out carefully. She'd taken Florrie to see one of the cheerful wartime movies that were supposed to make everyone forget their troubles for a little while. They'd both known why they were going out, but pretended that they didn't. They'd sat through the film, singing and laughing and joining in. But when they were quietly walking home together, Joyce had slipped her arm through Florrie's.

"Mrs. Pet has been, hasn't she?" Florrie said.

"Yes."

"And William has gone, hasn't he?"

"Yes," said Joyce.

And then they cried.

CHAPTER **13**

The best waves were in the autumn and the spring and, as the worst winter weather arrived, even the toughest surfers gave up. The wet-suit-hire van stopped coming, and the pier and the sands were left to the freezing gray sea.

Christmas came, and Florrie brought a wonderful home-made pudding down to Seaview Guest House and shared their Christmas dinner.

Matt didn't see so much of Florrie through the colder months. She didn't have her usual energy and she told Matt, jokingly, that she was hibernating. He could see through her little jokes, though, and he knew that some of her anxiety about falling had returned, with the streets covered in ice and Silver Street being quite a hill. She was always glad when he called in on her to relate the latest Seaburn gossip.

March was as cold as it could be, and Matt was desperate for the surfing gang to get going. He nagged Jennifer Stonehouse, but she looked at him as though he was mad.

"What? In this weather? You'd have to break the ice to get in."

Each morning, as Matt walked to school, he passed the Free-brough bus. Sometimes it was just pulling into the station. Sometimes it was pulling out. He could tell whether he was early or late for school, depending on where the bus was. He'd had the idea of getting on the bus and going off to Freebrough, just to see it, just to find out what sort of place it was, but then he'd dismissed it as being stupid and just kept on down the road and in at the school gates. But one particular Monday, when he'd felt even less like facing school than usual, he'd stopped by the bus station and joined the queue for the Freebrough bus.

As he moved toward the driver, who was taking the money, he had a moment of panic. He didn't know how far it was or how long it would take to get there, and he'd only got his dinner money.

"Freebrough, please."

The driver looked at him and frowned. Matt thought he was going to tell him to get off to school. "Return, is it?"

"Oh . . . yes."

"Half-fare, is it?"

Matt nodded.

"Eighty pence."

Matt took the ticket, relieved, and went to the back of the bus. Then the panic returned. He wouldn't know when he'd got there. He almost got off again, but then he heard two women with large shopping bags asking for Freebrough, too, so he decided to keep his eye on them and get off when they did. The motor started up and the bus drew out of the station, taking away the chance of changing his mind.

He saw gangs of his friends dutifully going to school, and

his stomach lurched. Still time to leap off the bus and join them. He turned his head away from the window, hoping that none of them would notice him. He stayed like that until the bus was well out of Seaburn and rattling past the steelworks, and villages, then through country lanes, away from the sea.

Matt felt good. Once he was safely away from Seaburn, a wild sense of freedom came to him. He was a prisoner escaping from the prison camp, he was a criminal on the run.

Almost an hour had passed before the bus pulled into a market town, and Matt saw that the two women with bags were getting restless in their seats, gathering their things together. The bus stopped and the driver called out, "Freebrough marketplace." Matt needn't have worried about missing his stop.

Freebrough was about the same size as Seaburn Bay. Matt walked round the market, enjoying the noise and the bustle. But then he reminded himself why he'd come, and he wandered off down neat streets with organized gardens, past small rows of shops. He looked at people as they came out of houses, especially at young women. Then he stopped. She wouldn't be young anymore. Well . . . she wouldn't be a young girl, she'd be about thirty. She might be married; she might have some other children by now. Then he started to notice women with prams and pushchairs and screaming toddlers having tantrums in the street. He walked on and on, turning corner after corner. The houses were getting more modern, and some of them were big. He still went on, looking at house after house until he was dizzy.

Suddenly he stopped.

He was tired and hungry. He didn't know what he was doing there. He couldn't find her, he knew that. He didn't know her address. She probably didn't even live in Freebrough anymore. He looked around at the smart houses on the street. It was all right. It wasn't a bad place. It was just that . . . well, there was something missing. It was too quiet. The air didn't smell right. The air didn't smell of anything at all. He grinned. That was it. There were no seagulls screaming their background chorus, no distant sound of the wash of waves. How did they live here, without all that? Without the sea?

It wasn't his place. It wasn't home.

Matt stared blankly in front of him at the freshly painted gate and the low, red-brick garden wall. He looked one way down the street, then turned and looked the other. He hadn't a clue which way he'd come. He didn't feel bothered about it, just stupid. He was completely lost and he couldn't think how he'd ever find a bus to take him back to Seaburn Bay. Then his brain started to work again. Yes, of course, the bus had stopped at the marketplace. It would be bound to pick up from there, too. He crossed the road to where a woman with a baby in a pushchair was coming down her garden path. He hesitated for a moment, then asked her the way to the marketplace. She had light brown, wavy hair, the same color as his, and pink cheeks and a kind smile. She gave him directions clearly, and touched his arm as she pointed and explained.

She was nice, he thought as he went off down the street. It isn't her, of course, but she's nice. My first mother might be like that. It didn't seem to matter much now. All he wanted was to get back to Seaburn Bay. Back to his mum and dad and Florrie and the wonderful smell of the sea.

He found the bus stop easily and bought himself a bar of chocolate and an apple, which he ate while he waited for the bus to come. By the time he got back to Seaburn, it was almost half past three. To fill in a few minutes before he went home, he walked round the top prom and past the cliff lift, breathing in deep lungfuls of cold, frosty air. As he turned the corner by the steps of the Grand, he thought he saw a black dot bobbing about in the sea, down by the pier. He ran across the road, straining to see better. Yes. They were there. Only a few of them, and no tea van or hire van, but they were there, fighting their way through the waves. The surfing gang had returned.

Matt hadn't planned to tell anyone about his visit to Freebrough, but somehow, surprisingly, he ended up telling his dad.

They'd gone for a walk up on Highcliffe that evening. Matt's dad had asked him if he wanted to come, just out of habit, and been amazed when Matt said yes.

"Smell that wind," his father teased, as they climbed up the steep, bracken-covered hillside. "Breathe in the sea air. Look at that sunset, lad." He waited for Matt's usual bored response of "Yeah, yeah, yeah."

But instead of that, Matt was suddenly telling him what he'd done.

His father didn't go mad at him for missing school. He listened quietly and nodded his head and said, "Did you now . . . aye."

When they reached the top, they crouched in the heather, watching the waves working their way in, steadily eating up the sand.

"It'll be on the turn in a few minutes," said Matt's dad. Matt nodded.

"You know, Matt, I'd rather have you than any other kid."

Matt smiled. "Would you, Dad?"

"I would."

There was another moment of quiet between them, then Matt spoke. It was hard to say it right, so that the words wouldn't hurt. "I'm glad that I'm with you, and Mam, too. It's just that . . . it's just that I can't quite get rid of this feeling of. . . ." He stopped. The words wouldn't come out right.

"What? Feeling of what?"

"It's a kind of sadness. That's what it is. Sadness about it all. You and Mam wanting a baby for so long and not being able to have one. Then there's her . . . the girl from Freebrough. Her having a baby and feeling that she had to give it away. Then there's Florrie. Florrie and her William."

"Aye. I do see what you mean. We are all people who've had something go wrong for us. There is sadness in that. To my way of thinking, there's nowt wrong in feeling it. A bit of sadness is only right."

Matt pushed his hand through his dad's arm and leaned against his shoulder. How come his dad, who said so little, sometimes said the most sensible things? The tension of worrying about it seemed to melt away. A bit of sadness was quite all right.

CHAPTER 14

Jennifer Stonehouse came rushing in at the school gate.

"Matt," she shouted. "Matt, come here. Quick."

Matt gaped at her. It was lunchtime, and he couldn't think why she'd suddenly want him, when she'd been ignoring him every time he tried to get her talking about surfing.

"Come on," she said, and grabbed him by the arm. "Quick. It's your auntie."

"What? Florrie?"

"Come on. She's got something for you."

Jennifer pulled him out through the school gates and along High Street.

Catcalls followed, from Wayne and the other kids who Matt had been playing football with.

"What is it? Dragging me off like this."

"You'll see. In here, in the church hall . . . not the front, round the back."

Matt saw that the old folks were beginning to fill up the church hall, ready for their afternoon club. He couldn't imagine what Florrie could be doing, hiding away round the back. Then he turned the corner and saw her. She was standing among piles of junk. Old rolled-up carpets, worn chairs, faded lamp shades, tables piled high with chipped china. She stood right in the middle, clutching on to a grubby, but decent and perfectly usable, surfboard.

"Wow! Where did you get that?"

"Sh!" Florrie put her finger to her lips and looked around like a nervous conspirator. "Come over here, and keep your voice down."

Matt stood there grinning.

"Go on, then," Jennifer gave him a shove.

Matt stepped carefully round the pots and bits and pieces.

"There now," said Florrie, pushing it forward. "What do you think?"

"What, me? Is it for me? Can I have it?"

"Of course you can. That's the idea. Pulled it out of the jumble-sale stuff. I spied it as soon as I came in. Not supposed to do this, of course, but I've given Mrs. Turvy fifty pence. She doesn't mind, but the vicar might. Well. Is it any good?"

Matt stroked the board with his hand.

"It's a good one," said Jennifer. "They're some of the best, these old ones, good and strong; bit heavier, but nice and steady. Worth more than fifty pence."

"It's fabulous," said Matt.

Florrie grinned. "Needs a bit of filling here, got a bit of a puncture . . . what do you call it?"

"A ding," said Matt, pressing his fingertips gently on the place.

"Your dad will help you to fix that. Here, you take it off me," and as he took hold, she put her hand to her mouth and started coughing.

Her face went all red and her eyes watery, but between the

coughing she told him, "Get off home and take the board round the back of your house, before the vicar comes."

Matt did as he was told, but he didn't like the sound of Florrie's cough at all.

"You get on," said Jennifer, still sounding somehow grumpy with him. "I'll take your auntie into the hall and get her a cup of tea."

Matt almost ran down Silver Street and down the side of his house. His mother saw him from the kitchen window and came nosying out.

"Wherever has that come from?"

"Church jumble sale."

"Jumble sale? But it isn't till Saturday."

"No. Florrie pulled it out of the jumble before it got sorted. She gave Mrs. Turvy fifty pence, so it's all right."

"Oh, that Florrie," his mother said, laughing. "She's a wicked one."

"Yeah, she is. She's got a nasty cough, though."

"Has she?" His mother frowned. "I'll pop up to see her later on."

That afternoon, Matt looked out for Jennifer coming back into the classroom. She walked into the room with a large carrier bag, her face like thunder.

"Hey," he said, leaning out across the row of desks, grinning and clicking his fingers at her. "Hey, hey, I've got a surfboard."

She looked straight at him, more furious than ever, and dumped the carrier bag down on his table.

"You've got a wet suit, too," she said, and marched off to sit at the back of the room.

113

Matt stared after her, his mouth open. He turned back and looked inside the bag. It was her yellow wet suit. He turned back to catch her eye, but she wouldn't look at him. Just then the teacher came into the classroom and banged on the desk for silence. There was nothing that Matt could do but put the bag carefully down on the floor and make an effort to take in what the teacher was saying.

He tried to catch Jennifer between lessons, but she seemed to be rushing ahead all the time, and it was only at hometime that he eventually managed to grab her.

"What's up?" he asked. "Why have you given me this?"

She stopped at last and sighed. She shrugged her shoulders. "It's no good to me."

Matt looked down at the suit, puzzled. "Why not? It's a good one."

She folded her hands across her chest. "Doesn't fit me anymore."

"Ey? Doesn't fit? You've not grown that much, have you? You're no taller than me."

She went red in the face and scowled down at the floor. "There's other ways of growing, thicko. Not that you'd notice. All you care about is the stupid surfing gang. Well, you've got all the gear you need now, so you can get on with it, can't you?"

She pulled herself away from him and went charging ahead, down High Street. He stared after her, shocked, suddenly seeing what she meant. The slim, straight body that he'd mistaken for a lad had changed. Her hips were rounded, and her waist went in . . . it went right in.

He let her go. It didn't seem the right moment to go chasing after her, and he wanted to have a bit of time to think about what she'd said. She'd been right to call him "thicko." A slow smile spread across his face. He remembered the time that he'd grabbed her hair by accident, and been surprised by the soft silkiness of it. He was a thicko, all right.

Matt couldn't get to sleep that night. He couldn't seem to get comfortable, and his mind was whizzing from one thing to another. He saw himself in the yellow wet suit, riding the waves on his sanded and newly repaired surfboard. Then he saw Jennifer angry and upset. Why was she so angry? Okay, so she needed a new wet suit. Her dad would buy her one. They were quite well-off. Jennifer was never short of money or clothes.

Then his mind swung away from Jennifer and settled on Florrie for a moment. He saw Florrie coughing in the drafty yard behind the church hall. She shouldn't have hung around in there for so long. His mother had been up to see her that night and she'd come back looking concerned. She'd insisted that Florrie go to bed, and said that she'd ring the doctor herself and get him to visit in the morning.

"Doctor?" Matt had said. "Florrie can't stand doctors. She really must be feeling poorly if she'll have the doctor."

Still, thought Matt, she was a tough old bird. She'd survived so many other things, surely she'd survive a bit of a cough. And he took his mind back to the surfing gang. He was one of them now. He'd got all the gear.

It was during the lunch hour that Matt managed to speak to Jennifer again.

"Hey? Are you avoiding me?" he asked.

She sighed. She never used to be one of those girls that

were always sighing, but she seemed to be doing it a lot just now.

" 'Course I'm not avoiding you. Gave you a wet suit, didn't I?"

"Yeah, but you don't seem very happy about it. Look . . . I'll give you some money for it." Matt swallowed hard as he said it, because he had no idea where the money might come from.

"No." She shook her head. "Don't want anything for it. It's no good to me. My dad said I can do what I want with it."

"Thanks. I'm sorry you've grown out of it like you said, but . . . well, I think you look. . . ."

"Stop it." She suddenly punched him on the chest, and he reeled back, shocked. "That's it. That's just it. That's why my dad won't buy me another one. He says I've got too grown-up to be down there with that gang of lads."

"What?" said Matt rubbing at his chest. "He won't let you go surfing anymore?"

She shook her head.

"But you're great at it. You're one of the best."

"Shut up. Just shut up about it, will you?"

She folded her arms and leaned back on the brick yard wall, looking miserable.

"Look. Don't give up. Florrie thinks you're wonderful, the way you do it. She said that if she was young enough, she'd be like you, out on the waves."

Jennifer smiled at the thought.

"Hey, I've got an idea," said Matt. "Does your dad know Florrie? It seems as though nearly everyone does. I could get Florrie to have a word with him. She's very bossy, you know. She can make anyone do what she says."

Jennifer looked thoughtful, but she shook her head. "She'd have a job with my dad. My mum knows Florrie, though, and I think she'd let me carry on, if it wasn't for Dad. Mum has often said that she wished she'd had the chance to do things like surfing."

"Hey," he said, flicking her ponytail into her face. "I'll tell Florrie about it, and see what she says. I know she'll be on your side."

CHAPTER 15

Matt stopped at Florrie's house on his way home, but he couldn't seem to make her hear. He tried the door and found it locked, then he remembered that she'd not been well, and he went off quietly down the street.

"Can't make Florrie hear me," he said, dropping his bag down on the kitchen floor.

"No," said his mother, putting the iron down on its stand. "No, you won't."

Matt saw that she was worried and waiting to tell him something.

"What's up, then?"

"Well . . . you know that she was feeling poorly. The doctor came and he's sent her into Freebrough General. She's got pneumonia."

Matt stared.

"It's the best thing. They'll get her sorted out in there."

"But pneumonia? Isn't that serious?"

"It can be serious, but there's a lot they can do to help her get better."

"I want to go and see her," said Matt. "She won't like being in there."

" 'Course you do. I want to see her, too. We'll go on Saturday, go together."

Matt felt awkward, standing in the Freebrough bus queue with his mother, carrying a large bunch of daffodils and remembering the last time that he'd caught that bus. His mother seemed to sense it. She gave him a nudge.

"Your dad told me, you know."

Matt pulled a face.

"It's all right," she said, laughing, "I understand. I can see why you wanted to go to Freebrough. When you are older you can probably find her, if you really want to."

"What? How do you mean?"

"It's part of the law nowadays. You have to wait until you're eighteen, then you have the right to find out all you can about your first mother. You could go to see the adoption people; they would tell you what to do, and they would help you."

"Oh," said Matt, gone all unsure. "I don't know. I don't know if I should."

"You don't have to do it. Just wait and see how you feel when the time comes."

Matt stood quietly thinking about it, then he suddenly grinned. "I can't believe it. Neither you nor Dad has said anything about me wagging off school."

"Oh, well." She gently punched his cheek. "That was special. Start to make a habit of it, and we'll have plenty to say."

The bus drew up and they got on, settling down in seats near the back.

"Why have they sent Florrie to Freebrough General?" Matt asked his mother.

"You mean, instead of the cottage hospital?"

He nodded.

"It's because they'll have all the latest equipment there. They have a big ward that deals with chest infections. Best chance of getting her better, so the doctor seemed to think."

"She'll hate it, though. I think that's the hospital they took her friends to when she was little. They had diphtheria. They died."

Matt's mother looked thoughtful. "That's right. It used to be the fever hospital. It's all modernized now, though. It'll be quite different."

The bus rattled and bounced past the steelworks and out into the countryside, past landmarks that Matt recognized. Matt looked out of the window, then back at his mother, and noticed that she was smiling to herself.

"What is it? What's the secret joke?"

"Not a joke," she said. "Just remembering things. This isn't the first time you will have been in Freebrough General."

"Hey? Was I ill then?"

"Well, actually, it was Freebrough General that we got you from."

"How do you mean?"

"You'd been poorly, you'd had enteritis. That's a sort of stomach bug that can be really serious for tiny babies. So you'd spent the first six weeks of your life in hospital. They'd managed to get you better, and the social workers thought that it would be best if you came straight to us, rather than go to a foster mother first, like most adopted babies do."

"Huh. I never knew that."

"Just didn't think to tell you. I'll show you where it was; we'll probably pass the children's ward."

They went past Freebrough marketplace, staying on the bus as it went through the town. The hospital was a large, low, red-brick building that seemed to stretch for miles right out into the countryside. It had been built out there, beyond the houses, to cut down the risk of infection.

Large signs, with long complicated medical words on them, pointed in all directions. They meant nothing to Matt. His mother seemed to understand it all and she steered him through swinging doors and down long corridors. The daffodils he was carrying began to droop.

At last they reached the right ward and joined a group of visitors waiting to be let in. A fat-chested, gray-haired nurse, dressed in dark blue and wearing a tiny white cap, pushed the door open and announced, "No more than three at a bed, please."

She looked down her nose at Matt, putting her hand out to his shoulder.

"No children allowed in this ward."

Matt and his mother looked at each other, horrified. Another nurse came up with a notepad and pencil. She wore pale blue.

"Oh, he's a big lad, Sister."

"No children," the first nurse repeated. "That's the rule, Staff Nurse Columba. There are some nasty chest infections in this ward, and the patients need complete rest and quiet."

"Oh, he'd be very quiet," said Matt's mother, taking him by the arm. "He's a special friend, you see. He's ever so fond of the lady that we're visiting."

"I'm sorry. It's the rule. He must wait out here if you go in." She pointed to some metal-framed chairs out in the corridor.

Matt saw that his mother had gone red in the face; she was angry, unsure what to do.

"Stupid rules," he said, pushing the bunch of daffodils into her hands. "You go and see her. Stupid to come all this way and neither of us see her."

"Are you sure you'll be all right?"

"Go on, I'll wait here," he said, and he kicked one of the uncomfortable-looking canvas chairs.

Matt shuffled about on the chair, then stood up and paced up and down. The nurse in the pale blue uniform went past and winked at him. She was thin, skinny really, and her cap flapped loose at one side where her hairpin had slipped. It bobbed up and down as she sped away down the corridor. Matt stared after her, full of admiration. He'd never seen anyone move that fast and still be walking. She had the sort of face that made you want to smile.

Thank goodness for her, thought Matt. He hated to think of Florrie being looked after by that grumpy old bag with the turned-down mouth.

It was boring, waiting. He examined the polished linoleum and the blank walls painted light gray. He didn't like to think of Florrie in this place at all. Her house bloomed with colorful displays of polished ornaments and smelled of lavender wax. Even the smell of the hospital was disgusting: a nasty mixture of school dinners and disinfectant.

At last the visitors began to leave the ward, talking in whispers and looking relieved. Matt's mother came out and pushed her arm through his. They went off down the corridor together.

"She liked the daffodils," she said.

"Well? How is she? Is she nearly better?"

"She's tired. Quiet. You know, not got the energy to gossip."

Matt frowned. That didn't sound like Florrie.

"The sister says that the pneumonia is clearing up, though. She says that Florrie's much better."

"Is the sister that ratty one?"

"Mmm."

"I bet Florrie can't stand her."

"Well, I don't think the sister approved of Florrie much, either. Florrie likes the other nurse, though, the one in the pale blue. Her name's Columba, but Florrie insists on calling her Columbine."

Matt let his mother steer him around the corner and through some doors. Then they faced another long corridor, stretching ahead, exactly the same as the one that they'd left.

His mother laughed.

"Oh, this reminds me," she said. "The day that we got you. It was just like this. We came with the social worker and we walked down corridor after corridor, and each time we went through these swinging doors, I got all tense. I thought, this is it. Our baby. The one we've wanted for so long. But each time the swinging doors opened, there was another corridor to walk down instead."

"You did get there."

"Yes, of course we did. But it wasn't what I'd thought. They showed us into a room with a huge crib in it, and I thought the crib was empty. Then, when I looked carefully, I saw that there was a tiny bump in the bedclothes."

"That was me?"

"It was you. You were so small . . . small as a newborn baby, because you'd been poorly. A nurse picked you up and showed you to us. You were so small, she could hold you in one hand. Then she passed you over to your dad. I felt scared, but they made me hold you, and the social worker asked if we wanted to take you home. I nodded my head; I couldn't speak."

"So did you just walk off with me?"

His mother shook her head.

"I wanted just to walk off with you, but then there was this right old rigmarole. You see, you were wearing hospital clothes, and we'd brought clothes for you that me and your gran had made. The terrible thing was that they made *me* change your clothes and put the new ones on. Right there in front of them all, and I'd never dressed a baby before. They even made me change your nappy."

Matt giggled.

"As soon as I started to take your clothes off, you cried. You turned bright red in the face and screamed. I couldn't do it properly at all, my hands were shaking, and the nurses were crowding around us, laughing and giving advice."

Matt pulled a face. "It sounds awful. Didn't you want to change your mind and leave me there?"

His mother giggled. "No. I wanted to grab hold of you and run. I wanted to run away with you, past the nurses and the social worker, just run and run down the corridors and out into the sun. I couldn't do that, though. We'd spent such a long time trying to convince them that we were sane and decent and fit to be parents. So I just got on with it. The clothes were miles too big for you—they dangled down from your legs—and you screamed all the way through."

"Oh, look," she said, pointing to another large sign. "That's it. Pediatrics. That must be the ward down there. Look, this is the place."

More swinging doors guarded the entrance to the children's ward. Matt's mother went up to the doors and stopped.

"We shouldn't go in."

The doors swung open and they heard the roar of a crying baby as a nurse came out.

"Can I help you?"

"No." Matt's mother smiled and shook her head. They turned and went off to follow the signs that said EXIT.

CHAPTER **16**

Three weeks passed. Matt's mother went off to visit Florrie every Wednesday and every Sunday. There wasn't any point in her specially going at weekends, as they wouldn't let Matt in. Each time she returned she gave good reports of Florrie and what the doctors had said.

The weather improved, and Matt and his dad worked on his surfboard. They repaired the ding with foam and fiberglass. Then they painted it with resin, sanded it well, and finished with a coat of gloss. The board was as good as new.

After that, Matt spent his weekends enjoying the sharp sunlight and the fierce spring tides, down by the pier with the surfing gang.

The first time he'd gone down with his surfboard and suit, he'd felt strange. There he was with all the gear, but Jennifer wasn't there, wittering on with her instructions, and there was no Florrie up on the pier, waving her arms about in wild encouragement.

Martin stopped and admired Matt's gear and told him that the waves were at their roughest at this time of the year. "Mind you, best surfing waves up the north coast, these are."

Matt struggled on, wading out and then riding back. He could feel that these waves were different. The strength of them could pick your feet up off the bottom and fling you down yards away. If only, he thought. If only I could get up on top of them and harness that energy, it would be fabulous. He put his weight carefully in the middle of the board, the way that Jennifer had shown him. Then, pushing up with his arms, he slowly slid his legs up until he crouched on the board, carried forward, lurching and swinging, but hanging on. For a moment he was up there, where he wanted to be, but the board tipped and juddered. He slipped to the side and crashed down into the angry sea.

Martin hauled him up. "Push-ups," he said.

"What?" Matt gasped, spouting water.

"Push-ups," Martin repeated. "That'll do the trick. You want to get that board wedged in a pile of sand, nice and steady. Then practice your push-ups on it. Give you muscles in all the right places, so that you can pull yourself up good and smooth and fast."

He clapped Matt on the shoulder and went striding out again. Matt stared after him. "Push-ups?" he repeated to himself.

"Hey, Matt! Hey, look."

Matt, scrabbling around in wet shingle to regain his board, looked up to see Wayne leaning over the edge of the pier.

"Hey, Matt. Look at this then. Got our Martin's old wet suit."

"Gonna come surfin' then?"

"Nay. Gonna jump off the pier. That's the daring thing to do, you know."

Matt watched, horrified, as Wayne climbed precariously over the railings and teetered on the edge.

"Hey," Matt yelled. "You gotta learn to swim first."

Wayne looked down at the waves as they bashed against the iron supports of the pier, flinging white spray so high that it splashed into his face. He grabbed tight onto the railings and clung to them.

"You gonna show me, then?"

"Yeah. Come down here."

Matt set his surfboard aside for a while and dragged Wayne further up the beach to the quieter end, where the waves were calmer, and struggled to get him to float. It was hard going, and Wayne was all for them going off to the swimming pool, but Matt yelled at him and shoved him about and insisted that he had to learn in the sea, if he wanted to jump off the pier. They kept at it for almost an hour, but by then Matt had run out of patience, and his stomach was growling for fish and chips.

As they plodded back toward the pier, Matt thought he saw Jennifer. He stopped and grinned. Yes, it *was* her. He wanted to laugh, but he stopped himself. She was up on her surfboard, carried along above a giant wave, her hair flapping wet down her back. She wore a black tracksuit top and her navy-blue school gym skirt, all soaking wet. He ran toward her and, as she tumbled down into the foam, he caught up with her.

"What you doing? Thought you couldn't come."

She fished her surfboard out of the water and pounded, dripping and determined, up the beach.

"He can't stop me. I'm doing it whether he likes it or not."

"What has your dad said, though? Does he know you've come?"

"Oh, yes. He knows, he went shouting down the street after me, but I don't care. I don't care if he hits me. My mam's on my side now, after he'd shouted at her that she was bringing her daughter up to be a tart."

"He said that?"

"Yes. My mam was furious and she said that she's bringing her daughter up to be tough. So I'm going to stick at it. I remembered how your Auntie Florrie wished she could have done it. Well, she really is too old, but I'm not."

Matt propped his surfboard up on an old heap of grubby builders' sand in his backyard. He kept glancing back at the kitchen windows to see if anyone was watching him. He wasn't quite sure if Martin had been joking. He felt stupid, but he could see that perhaps it could help. He got the board wedged firmly, with sand heaped up beneath it so that it was fairly level, just slightly tilted up at the nose.

He leaned forward, gripping the sides, then carefully pulled himself further forward and up. His arms wobbled and gave way. He crashed down, banging his nose on the board. His dad came round the side of the house as he rolled down to the ground, rubbing his nose.

His dad laughed. "What's up?"

Matt explained what Martin had said, and gave another demonstration.

His dad watched him levering himself up and down.

"That could work," he said.

The days went by, and as the warmer weather came, the visitors began to arrive. Seaburn became busier. Matt felt that a lot of things were happening, and they seemed to be happening fast.

There was Jennifer, for a start, looking smashing in the new red wet suit that her mother had bought from the mail-order catalog. Her dad had stopped shouting and given in, though he warned that trouble would come of letting a girl carry on as though she were a lad.

Then there was the news about the Grand Hotel. Seaburn Bay was buzzing with snippets of information. First they heard that the hotel had been sold to some businessman from the south who was going to pull it down and build flats. Then that was contradicted. No, he wasn't going to pull it down, he was going to do it up and have the enormous old rooms made into flats that could be sold off. At last the news came through clear and Matt heard it from his dad. The old hotel was to be turned into luxury flats that were all to be fitted out in Victorian style. Harry Metcalfe had been given the job of site agent and he'd immediately taken Matt's dad on, full-time. He'd been snapped up, for Harry knew him to be a good worker, and a craftsman.

The other thing that seemed to lead on from all that was Mrs. Teesdale's idea for the school play. She'd got together with the drama teacher and the music teacher and persuaded them that they should support Seaburn Bay in promoting its history by putting on a revival of the old pierrot show. She'd gotten her students all searching through their grannies' photograph albums and kids had been turning up at school with pictures of the pierrots, their peculiar pom-pom costumes, and old people's stories of the songs and the dances and the funny turns that they did.

Mrs. Teesdale kept asking Matt about Florrie because, she said, it was the homework Matt had done with Florrie that had started the whole idea off in her head.

"We need your auntie. We need her advice. How long is it that's she's been in hospital now?"

"It's nearly six weeks, I think."

"You tell her that, tell her that we need her, next time you go to visit her."

"Not allowed to visit her," Matt said. "Don't let kids in that ward."

"Oh." Mrs. Teesdale suddenly looked concerned. "I'm sorry about that, Matt. A visit from you might be just what she needs."

CHAPTER 17

Matt worked out a fitness routine. Each morning and evening he did twenty push-ups. He practiced moving from lying on his belly to the kneeling position, then quickly up to the standing position, knees bent, ready to adjust his balance. He worked and worked on it, until he could feel new strength in his shoulders and arms, finding enjoyment in the exercise so that he almost forgot the purpose of it all.

His mother kept up her visits to the hospital, but each time she returned, she seemed more worried.

"When is she coming out?" Matt demanded. "Surely she should be better by now."

His mother sighed and shook her head. "Sometimes it's not quite as simple as that, love. They say that she's better, that the pneumonia has gone, but it's left her very weak and . . . well, exhausted. She isn't herself, Matt. I can hardly get a word out of her, and when she does talk, she seems to be getting all bothered and anxious about silly little things. She was going on the other day about some tin that's in one of her cupboards at home. Saying that she wants you to have it. I sometimes wonder. . . ."

"What? The tin? She isn't going to die, is she?"

"No. No . . . I don't think so. It's just that she can't seem to get herself going again, and I'm afraid that she might be there for a long time. There are other old women in that ward, they've been there for months, sometimes even years, and it's such a dismal ward, so . . . depressing."

"Yes," said Matt. "I could tell that it was like that, even though that disgusting woman wouldn't let me in. The smell was horrible, and Florrie . . . Florrie loves nice smells, especially lavender; that's what she really likes."

Matt walked slowly up Silver Street and crossed the road by the bus station on his way to school. Despite all the good things that were happening, he felt miserable. It was a growing kind of misery that slowly got worse, and it was all to do with Florrie. It was quite different from the gentle feeling of sadness that he'd talked to his father about. That was a sadness for things long ago, that you couldn't do anything to change. This was a sharp, nagging frustration because, somewhere at the back of his mind, he knew that something should be done. Action should be taken. But what action, and who should take it? Nobody seemed to be making enough fuss. He couldn't charge into the hospital like an olden-days' hero and rescue her from that dreadful dragon nurse who wore navy blue. He almost laughed at the thought.

He stopped. The Freebrough bus was just pulling into the bus station and the people in the queue were picking up their bags. No, he couldn't do that again. Besides, he'd got history today, and what with all the research they were doing about the pierrot shows, history was getting quite interesting. He walked on a few more paces, down the road toward his

133

school, but then he stopped again. What had Mrs. Teesdale said to him? "A visit from you might be just what she needs." Well, she had said that, hadn't she? Right. That was what he was going to do. He put his hand in his pocket. Yes, he'd got enough money . . . just about. He turned and walked straight toward the bus queue. People were beginning to climb on. He moved slowly forward, but as he passed the florist's shop, the one with the stupid name—The Flower Bowl—he got another idea. He left the queue and went inside.

"Have you got any lavender?"

The girl looked blank, then shook her head.

"Sorry, love. We sometimes have it dried, but we're out of it at the moment."

Matt went back outside. The last few people were getting on the bus, but it didn't usually pull straight out. He shoved open the door of the chemist's shop next to the florist's.

"Have you got some scent that smells of lavender?"

The woman smiled and nodded. She put three bottles of varying sizes out on the counter.

"There's the perfume, then there's the cologne, then there's lavender water."

Matt counted his money, trying to think fast. After he'd paid the bus fare, he'd only have eighty pence. He hadn't got enough, not even for the smallest bottle.

"Sorry," he said and turned away. The woman sighed and began returning the bottles to their shelves.

It was just as he was going out of the door that he saw it. It was part of a small display of cleaning materials. Brasso, dusters, turpentine, and a small round tin of furniture polish—lavender wax. Matt grabbed it; he could hear the engine starting up on the bus. Lavender wax, fifty pence.

"This is it." He turned to the woman, holding it out. "This is what I want, and I've got to get that bus."

The shop woman made a "huh" sound, but she gave him his change quickly, and he rushed out of the shop, jumping onto the bus as it was beginning to move.

Matt flopped down, out of breath, on the backseat of the bus. He spent the journey staring out at the countryside that was beginning to feel familiar, while a disturbing conversation with himself went on inside his head. Was he going mad? He'd done it now, he'd missed school. He'd really done something crazy this time. After all, even if he could find his way to the right ward, without his mother to work it all out, they weren't going to let him in, were they? He looked down at the tin of polish that he clutched in his hand. That was the stupidest thing of all. People took grapes, or flowers, and the perfume idea would have been okay, but polish . . . a tin of polish. He must be cracking up!

When the bus stopped in Freebrough marketplace, he got to his feet. He'd just enough money for a bar of chocolate. He could get himself a bar of chocolate and wander round the stalls for a bit. One of the market traders was shouting and clattering plates as a crowd gathered. It all sounded noisy and interesting. He walked down the aisle of the bus, but hesitated just as it was his turn to step down.

The driver revved the engine and looked at him.

"Getting off or not?"

"Sorry," he said. "Sorry, wrong stop. Want the hospital."

"Righto then. Two more stops yet. Better sit yourself down again."

Matt swung himself into the nearest seat as the bus pulled

out and lurched round the corner. He put the tin of polish into his pocket, feeling foolish, but somehow glad that he hadn't actually gotten off. After all, he told himself, he'd only go back to being miserable again. He'd only go back to that feeling of wanting to do something, but not actually bothering. Nothing could be worse than that. At least he could have a try. He could go to the hospital and see if there was any way he could possibly get in. There was that kind nurse, the skinny one who'd winked at him . . . if he could just find her.

Florrie lay in the neat hospital bed with her eyes closed and her head turned to the side. She looked as though she was asleep, but she wasn't; her eyes were simply closed against the glare of the lights.

There was a rattling of cups and saucers as the tea trolley was pushed rumbling down the ward. A plump auxiliary nurse plonked a cup of tea down on the small formica-topped locker beside her bed.

"Come on, love, drink your tea, there's a pet. We're late this morning and we've got to be cleared before the doctors come."

She hurried on to the next bed.

Florrie opened her eyes and began the slow struggle to sit up. She looked round at Elsie, who was in the next bed. The nurse was letting down the big cot side with a clank. She heaved the old woman up against the pillows, holding the feeding cup up to the slack mouth.

"Come on now, Elsie. Try, love. We've got to be getting a move on."

Elsie moaned, and made slurping noises in her efforts to drink fast.

"Oh dear, Elsie, you're not wet again, are you?"

Elsie moaned and said something in a squeaky little voice that Florrie could not hear properly.

The nurse spoke in a louder voice. "I say you're wet again, aren't you, Elsie?" Then she shouted down the ward. "One here to change, Nurse."

Florrie turned her head and looked across at Phyllis, the woman in the bed directly opposite her.

Phyllis shook her head and mouthed some words to Florrie, but Florrie was too far away either to hear what she said or see her lips clearly. A strong smell of urine drifted over to Florrie's bed. She looked at her cup of tea and suddenly felt sick. She lowered herself until she was lying down again and closed her eyes, turning her head away from Elsie's bed.

The thin nurse who wore pale blue came to take Florrie's cup. She frowned as she picked it up.

"You've not drunk your tea again, Florrie. Are you feeling poorly, darlin'?"

Florrie opened her eyes; she gave a weak smile. "Oh, it's you, Columbine. I'm sorry. I just can't seem to fancy it."

Columbine bent over the bed and whispered, "I don't blame you darlin', it's just like dishwater. Not like you make at home, ey? Still, you should try, you know. Got to keep your fluids up, then you can get out of this place. Make your own tea at home."

She turned back, smiling, but she saw that Florrie's eyes were closed, that she wasn't listening. The smile went, and she pressed her lips tight together with concern as she moved on to fetch Elsie's cup.

*   *   *

Sister Walker and the consultant began their parade down the ward, stopping for a moment at each bed. They were followed by two doctors and a trickle of medical students. Florrie kept her eyes tightly shut, pretending to sleep again, and they did not disturb her. Sister Walker gave a slight, hopeless shrug of her shoulders and passed on to Elsie. Columbine hovered behind them until they had moved on from Elsie and drawn the curtains around the next bed. Then, with a fast and decisive movement, she drew Florrie's curtains.

Florrie opened her eyes, puzzled.

Columbine bent down and whispered close to Florrie's ear, "Pretend I'm bringing you a bedpan."

"Ey?" Florrie spoke sharp. "I don't want any bedpan. Can't stand the things."

"Sh." Columbine put her finger to her lips and looked fierce. "I'm not really bringing you one. I'm going to fetch you a visitor. It's that young lad you told me about. The one who's mad on surfing."

"What? You mean Matt?"

Columbine nodded. "I've hidden him in the day-care room. Now just keep quiet, and when they've moved on to Mrs. Hutchins, I'll bring him through."

Florrie frowned and shook her head. "No. Can't be Matt . . . not here. You'll get yourself into trouble, my girl."

"No I won't," Columbine told her firmly. "You know what they're like. When they get down to the end, they move on to the men's ward. Sister Walker won't be back for half an hour."

"Oh . . . I don't know," Florrie looked uncomfortable. "I don't like the thought of Matt in this place."

"Well, I think it'll do you good to see him. And I can tell

you this, I'm not sending him away. Poor lad, he's skipped off school to come here, and he's had a terrible job finding the ward. The only name he could remember was Pediatrics, and he ended up in the babies ward. Luckily Sister Welford showed him up here. I'm not sending him away after all that. Sit yourself up; I'm going to get him now."

CHAPTER 18

Matt tried to push down the sick, panicky feeling in his stomach as the door to the day-care room opened. He was ready to run, but then, with relief, he saw that it was Columbine.

"Come on, then, quick and quiet, or you'll get me fired."

He put his hand in his pocket. His fingers closed around the tin of polish. He gripped it tight as he followed Columbine's swishing blue skirt through the swinging doors and past another nurse, who grinned at him. He had only a quick impression of the vast expanse of brightly lit ward before Columbine thrust him through the drawn curtains and he found himself standing at the foot of Florrie's bed.

He stood there for a moment, blinking and shocked. Florrie was propped up in bed, leaning back against the pillows. Matt thought she looked dreadful. Her face was yellow and thin, with blue shadows showing beneath the cheekbones. The fine white hair that she used to spend so much time combing and patting into neat curls stood up in alarming tufts around her head. Was this really Florrie? Florrie who wouldn't leave the house without powdering her nose and applying a careful touch of pink lipstick?

They stared at each other in silence.

Columbine stuck her head through the curtains and hissed. "Quiet, remember. Keep it quiet. Five minutes, then you gotta go, darlin'."

Matt had been planning the things that he would say. He'd meant to tell Florrie about all the interesting things that were going on in Seaburn. He'd planned to tell about Jennifer, and the Grand Hotel, and the plans for the pierrot show, but somehow the sight of Florrie had wiped all those things from his mind.

She looked pitiful. But a small spike of anger broke through his pity. She'd no business lying there in the hospital bed looking like that. He needed her.

"What are you doing?" He almost shouted it. "You aren't getting better. Why not?"

"Quiet," Florrie hissed at him. "Get us all into trouble, you will." She heaved herself up higher on the bed.

"Sorry." Matt jumped and glanced nervously behind him. Then he whispered. "Sorry . . . but you aren't getting better, are you? You don't even seem to be trying."

Florrie didn't answer. She turned her head away from him and sighed.

"I can't understand it," his voice slowly rose above a whisper. "You are the one who's always going on about never giving up. Look at you now, you've given up completely. That was rubbish, all that stuff you told me. All that about . . . riding the waves. 'They can knock you down,' that's what you said, 'but they can't stop you getting back up there and trying again.'"

Florrie looked back at him, angry now.

"Well? And have you done it yet? Have you been riding the waves? Have you got up on that surfboard yet and stayed there?"

Matt's mouth opened, but he didn't answer.

"Well then, don't you go lecturing me, my lad."

The curtains shook and Columbine's head appeared again.

"Out," she said. "Get out. I'm not having that shouting going on."

"I'm going," Matt said. Then he remembered the polish. He fished in his pocket and plonked it down on Florrie's bedside locker.

"I had a lot to tell you," he said. "I had loads of news and gossip, but I'm not telling you now. You don't have to die, you know. You don't have to die just because you've come in here. You haven't got diphtheria. You're the one who used to be a nurse. You should know. As a matter of fact, I came from this hospital. This is where they got me from. I didn't die." And he went, the curtains swishing together behind him.

Columbine followed him out. She shoved him through the swinging doors and watched as he ran down the long corridor. Even after he'd gone, she stayed there staring at the empty space for a moment, then she nodded her head and smiled.

Columbine didn't speak as she slowly opened the curtains that surrounded Florrie's bed. Florrie was lying down. She was very still, but her eyes were wide open, staring up at the hospital lights.

She blinked a couple of times and looked at Columbine. Then she suddenly sat up in bed and started pulling open the locker door in an agitated way.

"What is it?" Columbine asked. "What's the matter? What do you want?"

Florrie didn't answer. She pulled a small mirror and a comb out of her locker, then she noticed the tin of lavender polish and picked it up. She looked at it for a moment, puzzled, then began fiddling with the catch at the side. The lid came off and rolled under the bed. Columbine watched as Florrie held the small tin up to her nose and breathed in deeply. Florrie smiled, then she laughed.

"All right," she said. "All right, my lad. You win."

She pushed back the bedclothes, swinging her legs to the side.

"What are you up to now?" asked Columbine.

Florrie looked at her, surprised. "Haven't you got a polish cloth? And I could do with a nice clean duster."

Columbine frowned.

"I can't do much with this chipped formica top, but the rest of it is good wood. It'll come up lovely when I've had a go at it. Now then, did I bring any lipstick in here with me? Pink orchid, that's the one I like. Well, my girl? Are you going to stand there all day? Have you got a cloth?"

Columbine grinned. "For you, my darlin', anything."

It was two o'clock in the afternoon. The beach was almost deserted, just one old man walking his dog around the rock pools beneath Highcliffe.

Matt crossed the top prom. He was dressed in his wet suit and carried his surfboard. He stopped at the top of the bank and looked down at the empty beach and the rough sea.

"How dare she?" He whispered it under his breath. "How dare she?"

He set off, running and slithering down the bank, losing hold of his surfboard so that it thumped through the grass ahead of him. He picked it up at the bottom and, tucking it under his arm, he charged across the bottom prom and down the cobbled slipway, like a knight carrying his lance into battle. He ran down the beach toward the waves, stubbing his feet against the rocks and pebbles.

The water was freezing cold, and a strong offshore wind blew against the waves so that they lashed themselves like whips toward the sand. Sharp spring sunlight cut through the clouds in streaks and dazzled his eyes. He stopped, gasping for breath as the sea washed round his ankles. He looked up and down the empty beach.

"You could drown in this sea," he said out loud. "You could drown here, and nobody would save you or even see."

Then he ploughed forward into the waves, his face bright with anger and his body filled with power.

He waded out beyond the white surf, then gripped the board, looking for a wave. It came rolling toward him.

"Now," he yelled. "Now."

He pushed off and paddled like mad. His stomach lurched with delight as he felt the wave lift his board. He closed his eyes and made himself think of his own backyard and the endless push-ups. He gritted his teeth and swung himself up smooth and fast into the kneeling position, then straight up, the muscles in his legs clenching tight. The board wobbled and tipped. He countered it and balanced, crouching low at first, then pushing himself up. And he was up there, tipping and swinging, but staying there, high above the fury of the sea.

He shouted aloud. Shouted to the cliffs and the seagulls and the empty beach.

"Hey, Florrie, I'm doing it! I'm doing it now! I'm riding the waves!"